T5-AGP-928

CANZONI VILLANESCHE
AND VILLANELLE

RECENT RESEARCHES IN THE MUSIC OF THE RENAISSANCE

James Haar, general editor

A-R Editions, Inc., publishes seven series of musicological editions
that present music brought to light in the course of current research:

Recent Researches in the Music of the Middle Ages and Early Renaissance
Charles M. Atkinson, general editor

Recent Researches in the Music of the Renaissance
James Haar, general editor

Recent Researches in the Music of the Baroque Era
Christoph Wolff, general editor

Recent Researches in the Music of the Classical Era
Eugene K. Wolf, general editor

Recent Researches in the Music of the Nineteenth and Early Twentieth Centuries
Rufus Hallmark and D. Kern Holoman, general editors

Recent Researches in American Music
H. Wiley Hitchcock, general editor

Recent Researches in the Oral Traditions of Music
Philip V. Bohlman, general editor

Each *Recent Researches* edition is devoted to works
by a single composer or to a single genre of composition.
The contents are chosen for their potential interest to scholars
and performers, then prepared for publication according to the
standards that govern the making of all reliable historical editions.

Subscribers to any of these series, as well as patrons of subscribing institutions,
are invited to apply for information about the "Copyright-Sharing Policy"
of A-R Editions, Inc., under which policy any part of an edition
may be reproduced free of charge for study or performance.

Address correspondence to

A-R EDITIONS, INC.
801 Deming Way
Madison, Wisconsin 53717

RECENT RESEARCHES IN THE MUSIC OF THE RENAISSANCE • VOLUMES 82–83

Orlando di Lasso et al.

CANZONI VILLANESCHE AND VILLANELLE

Edited by Donna G. Cardamone

A-R Editions, Inc.

Madison

For the University of Minnesota
Ensemble for Early Music

© 1991 by A-R Editions, Inc.
All rights reserved
Printed in the United States of America

Library of Congress Cataloging-in-Publication Data

Canzoni villanesche and villanelle.

(Recent researches in the music of the
Renaissance, ISSN 0486-123X ; v. 82–83)
   Vocal works for 3–4 voices.
   Italian words, also printed as texts with
English translations, p.   .
   Includes bibliographical references (p.   ).
   Contents: Villanesche from Lasso's "Opus 1"
(1555)—Neapolitan models for Lasso's
villanesche—Villanelle from Lasso's Libro de
villanelle (1581)—Neapolitan models for
Lasso's villanelle—Intabulations for lute—
Intabulations for four-course cittern—Intab-
ulations for six-course cittern—Intabulations
for keyboard.
   1. Villanelle (Part-songs) 2. Intabulations.
I. Cardamone, Donna G. II. Lasso, Orlando di,
1532–1594. Madrigali, vilanesche, canzoni
francesi, e motetti. Selections, 1991.
III. Lasso, Orlando di, 1532–1594. Libro de
villanelle, moresche, et altre canzoni. Selections. 1991. IV. Series.
M2.R2384 vol. 82–83   90-753037
ISBN 0-89579-245-1

Contents

LIBRARY
ALMA COLLEGE
ALMA, MICHIGAN

Neapolitan Models for Lasso's Villanelle

Intabulations for Lute

Intabulations for Four-Course Cittern

Preface

This anthology of sixteenth-century vocal and instrumental compositions has as its core Lasso's four-part *villanesche alla napolitana* from his "Opus I" of 1555 and four-part *villanelle* from his *Libro de villanelle* of 1581. These spirited dialect songs, which reflect Lasso's youthful enthusiasm for Neapolitan popular traditions and the comic arts of satire and deception, have delighted the musical public since 1898, when they appeared in the first edition of the composer's collected works.[1] The present edition takes some new approaches, particularly in regard to the texts. All strophes of multistrophic poems are underlaid to the music, and separate transcriptions of the texts, along with side-by-side translations and annotations clarifying dialectal elements, are provided in the Texts, Translations, and Commentary section. Edited here for the first time in complete form are the three-part *villanesche* that served as Lasso's models, as well as intabulations for lute, cittern, and keyboard of Lasso's four-part *villanesche*. The juxtaposition of interrelated compositions in one volume invites comparative study and suggests a variety of options in performance.

The Composer and His Music

Many details of Lasso's journeyman period (1544–54), the formative decade in which he composed his Neapolitan songs, have come into sharper focus owing to Horst Leuchtmann's authoritative biographical studies[2] and scholarship stimulated by the celebration in 1982 of the 450th anniversary of the composer's birth.[3] Expanding upon this new fund of knowledge, I have retraced Lasso's steps from boyhood to maturity and interpreted the social and cultural contexts in which his witty Neapolitan style originated.

The Imperial Circle

According to Lasso's first biographer, Samuel van Quickelberg, Lasso was born in Mons (Hainaut) in 1530, the same year in which Pope Clement VII confirmed the coronation of Charles V.[4] Although Lasso and the emperor may never have met, by the time the composer reached manhood his distinctive cosmopolitan character had been shaped by extensive travel through imperial lands and residence at Italian courts dominated by an aristocratic elite loyal to the crown. In Charles's struggle against France—the chief occupation of his life after 1521—he relied upon substantial revenues from the Netherlands and Italy, concentrating his efforts along this north–south axis and extending it northwestward by brief alliance with England. Lasso traversed this route between 1544 and 1554 under the protection of Italian nobles caught up in the emperor's ideal of Catholic supremacy in Europe. He returned north on the verge of adulthood at the very time Charles planned to abdicate, and submitted the fruits of his southern sojourn for publication in Antwerp. Duke Albrecht V of Bavaria engaged him as singer in his court chapel at Munich in 1556, and Lasso remained in service there—from 1563 as Kapellmeister—until his death in 1594.

Lasso's employers or traveling companions during the journeyman period included the imperial commander and statesman Ferrante Gonzaga; the literary dilettantes Constantino Castriota and the marchese della Terza; the exiled archbishop of Florence, Antonio Altoviti; and the professional soldier, singer, and actor Giulio Cesare Brancaccio. The noblemen who stood by Lasso in his youth composed a circle of "perfect" courtiers, schooled in warfare, attracted to military adventure, proficient in chivalry, and educated in the arts and letters. Their manners, artistic values, and political ambitions played an important role in Lasso's southern acculturation, as in turn they introduced him to social and class conditions in various regions of the Mediterranean world. Situating Lasso in relation to these men and their respective contexts brings insight into the gradual emergence of his true musical wit, at once ingenuous and amicably shrewd.

At about age twelve Lasso entered the service of Ferrante Gonzaga (1507–57), the third son of Isabella d'Este and Francesco II, marchese of Mantua. Gonzaga maintained his family's traditional allegiance to the empire through extensive service as commander in the imperial army, as viceroy of Sicily (1535–46), and as governor of Milan (1546–54). Military expeditions throughout the empire occupied much of his time, and he was nowhere more at home than in his encampments. His participation in artistic patronage was undistinguished, but he did have a genuine regard for the arts and letters, and his "noble spirit took pleasure in music."[5] Lasso consented to serve Gonzaga in 1544, after two earlier attempts to recruit him for his beautiful treble voice had failed. Quickelberg noted that at the time, "Gonzaga was commander-in-chief of the emperor's army at Saint-

Dizier, and he took Lasso away when the French invasions ended'' (September 1544).[6]

In December 1544 Gonzaga left Fontainebleau for Sicily to resume his position as viceroy. He was forced to stop at Mantua for the better part of 1545, however, because his wife had fallen gravely ill. His presence there can be documented from 1 January to 11 September.[7] During this extended sojourn Lasso would have made the acquaintance of court improvisers valued for their expert skills in singing impromptu verse and popular tunes to lute accompaniment. As solo singer in the service of a family long known for supporting the improvisatory arts, Lasso was surely encouraged to cultivate this extroverted style of entertainment.

Gonzaga's entourage eventually arrived at Palermo (by ship from Genoa) in November 1545, but he remained there only a few months because Charles V appointed him governor of Milan in March. Feudal ideals lay deep in Gonzaga's character, and as governor of Milan he was drawn toward a statecraft hinging on fealty to the crown and the concentration of Spanish military power in the Mediterranean basin. No Gonzaga prince was more conversant with Spanish customs than Ferrante, or as closely linked to the Spanish dominions of Charles V in southern Italy. Like the Spanish grandees with whom he associated, Ferrante was an arrogant, authoritarian figure, reputed even to have disarmed rebellious soldiers with one glance from his piercing black eyes (illus. 1).[8] Diplomatic dispatches are rife with descriptions of Gonzaga's displays of power, but they reveal some vulnerable moments of passion, too. The emperor once had to confine Gonzaga to his quarters after an altercation with a Spanish count (Feria) over a noblewoman.[9] Spanish domination of the greater part of the peninsula led to satirical characterization arising from hostility to the invaders. Figures like Gonzaga and Count Feria, caricatured as braggarts and vain womanizers, served as prototypes for the role of captain in Italian comedies. Having witnessed the mannerisms of such gallants in person and in stage roles, Lasso was prepared to parody their affectations and exaggerated sense of honor when they appeared as stock characters in Neapolitan song texts.

In Milan, Gonzaga maintained an instrumental ensemble and a small private *cappella* led by Hoste da Reggio, who was probably Lasso's first mentor in composition.[10] In 1548 the governor hosted two state visits from members of the imperial family.[11] Marked by an extravagant display of material and cultural wealth, these visits solidified his family's link to the empire, and Gonzaga spared no expense for the continuous rounds of banquets, tournaments, and comedies, the last staged with musical *intermedii* performed by mixed consorts of voices and instru-

Illus. 1. Portrait of Ferrante Gonzaga. Engraving from André Thevet, *Les vrais pourtraits et vies des hommes illustres* (Paris: I. Keruert and Guillaume Chaudiere, 1584), vol. 2, bk. 5, 412. Reproduced by permission of the Widener Library, Harvard University.

ments.[12] Lasso must have participated in these activities, for they clearly required all of his patron's artistic personnel.

The comedies then in repertory exploited a range of dialects and jargons characterizing social classes, and they featured realistic musical insertions in the main action, often popular tunes rendered in a derisive tone.[13] This was the spectrum of convivial theatrical entertainment that enjoyed an enthusiastic reception in Gonzaga's circle and led to Lasso's early command of Italian dialects and knowledge of stock comic roles. The first explicit evidence of Lasso's response is found in his Neapolitan dialect songs, which reveal a keen ear for the intonation of dialectal speech and an unerring sense of timing and mimicry born of identifying with the antics of Italian comedians.

By 1548 Lasso's voice was either changing or already a mature tenor,[14] prompting Gonzaga to release him shortly thereafter to pursue a musical career in Naples, where in early 1549 Lasso entered the service of Ferrante Gonzaga's brother-in-law, Giovan Battista d'Azzia, the marchese della Terza.[15] It is likely that Gonzaga transferred Lasso to d'Azzia's household on the basis of his familiarity with the marchese's musical needs, if not under pressure from his wife and his wife's sister Giulia, the marchesa della Terza, who may have wanted to keep Lasso in the family, so to speak. D'Azzia and Gonzaga maintained near-by residences in the Nido sector of Naples.[16] Both men were associated with the *sedile* Nido,[17] one of five district assemblies of noblemen responsible for electing deputies to the *giunta*, which administered the city government.[18] More often than not the headquarters of a *sedile* had the atmosphere of a social club where heads of baronial families "spent the whole day at leisure, occupied only with the exercise of arms and idle conversation."[19] Lasso's service as d'Azzia's household musician may well have been negotiated under these circumstances.

While in Naples Lasso experienced the kinds of entertainment to which Neapolitan patricians were most particularly disposed. Eyewitness accounts of Neapolitan festive occasions, though not exactly contemporary with Lasso's stay in Naples, nevertheless portray the customs of the aristocratic society Lasso aimed to please. Among the most informative are dispatches from a Mantuan ambassador, Count Nicola Maffei, who described in meticulous detail the festivities mounted by Neapolitan nobles on the occasion of Charles V's triumphal entry into Naples and sojourn there from November 1535 to March 1536. A scene of prosperity and cultural vitality was staged for the emperor's benefit. During the rounds of banquets, balls, jousts, bullfights, and comedy performances, Neapolitan nobles exhibited their richly adorned retinues, palaces, and gardens, the magnificence of which caused the Mantuan envoy—already accustomed to lavish displays of wealth and power—to react with astonishment and sincere admiration. The women rode about the city in elaborately trimmed carriages with jewel-studded side posts of silver. Attired in gleaming velvets and glowing silks, they were accompanied by large retinues of servants and pages in extravagant livery. Their palace chambers were furnished in voluptuous hangings of precious cloths that embodied a predilection for sensual pleasures. To Maffei, Neapolitan patricians had a "supreme arrogance, great ostentation, and excessive pride" ("una grandissima superbia, una gran pompa et extrema vanagloria").[20] No doubt luxury and wealth were vaunted in the extreme for the emperor's visit, but the spectacular show continued, and by the end of the century many nobles were impoverished and forced to sell their titles. Yet the expenditures incurred in exhibiting their material wealth did provide a means of sustenance for the lower classes of servants, artisans, and household musicians like Lasso.

Carnival was traditionally celebrated in Naples with a variety of outdoor activities to divert the crowds of roaming merrymakers. Maffei reported what the emperor witnessed when he toured the city on horseback at Shrovetide: courtesans flinging eggs filled with scented waters to masqueraders gathered beneath their windows; strolling minstrels improvising songs in honor of the lovely ladies whose windows they passed; groups of musicians stationed in various sections of the city competing with one another in singing *villanesche* and well-concerted madrigals.[21] The *villanesca* is essentially a serenade with an erotic or derisive message and hence appropriate to the wanton atmosphere of Carnival. Its companion form, the *mascherata* (masking song), recreates the impression of a Carnival scene and is always overtly addressed to ladies.[22] A company of maskers identifies a trade and then offers samples, thinly disguised as phallic metaphors, to flaunt masculine prowess. Lasso's *O belle, fusa!* (no. [15] in this edition), the salacious song of the spindlemakers, is the only *mascherata* in his repertory. It is an arrangement of an earlier piece by the Neapolitan poet-composer Gian Domenico da Nola, whose setting probably originated about the time of the emperor's visit (see no. [26]). Nola's poem satirizes a class of artisans vital to the Neapolitan economy, which depended in large measure on the export trade in silk goods and wool.

Lasso served as *musico*[23] in the d'Azzia household until fall 1551. His duties probably included performing at social gatherings and, as his stature grew, possibly giving music lessons. The retention of salaried household musicians by cultured noblemen or rich members of the *popolo* to entertain guests and to teach their children was a well-established Neapolitan tradition, particularly among families associated with the *seggio* Nido.[24] The reason why *musici di casa* were so valued in Nido is explained by Maffei, who noted that during the emperor's visit the most elegant parties were given at four or five homes there, graced by musical entertainment so striking that it "seemed paradise had disclosed every bit of its beauty and harmony" ("parea che el Paradiso havesse aperto ogni sua bellezza et armonia").[25]

Giovan Battista d'Azzia, whose branch of the family had come to Naples from Capua, descended from a long line of distinguished men-at-arms who won glory in wars fought for the kings of Naples without succumbing to the temptation of conspiring with the French. Like his forebears, he was widely respected for his knowledge of chivalry and letters.[26] He owned land in Terra di Otranto (Puglia), but it is not known if he supervised its workings.[27] D'Azzia flourished amid the hum of intellectual activity radiating from the northern zone of Naples where the noble families were concentrated (see plate 1). Nido was a small sector in this zone, and its noble families were characterized as "liberal," "open-minded," and "generous."[28] To d'Azzia must be attributed a fair share of influence in developing Lasso's perception of current literary trends. Lasso set one of his poems, "Euro gentil se d'amoroso ardore," in a "tentative style," which argues for an early date and supports the contention that he composed madrigals while living in Naples.[29] Testimony to d'Azzia's stature among *litterati* of his generation is found in books dedicated to him by the Venetian critics Lodovico Dolce and Girolamo Ruscelli. Various of his poems were published in Venetian anthologies of the 1550s, but he is best known for a platonic sonnet in praise of Maria d'Aragona (wife of Alfonso d'Avalos).[30] D'Azzia was among the founders in 1546 of the Accademia dei Sereni, whose aims were consonant with his humanistic interests. The membership of the Sereni, drawn from the nobility and *popolo*, gathered biweekly in a vaulted room on the ground floor of the Cortile Sant'Angelo for readings of literary works on predetermined topics and for lectures on philosophy, mathematics, and poetry.[31] A little more than a year after its establishment, the Accademia dei Sereni was dissolved by the viceroy of Naples, Pietro Toledo, who considered it a potential source of heresy and sedition. Despite its short existence, the academy was of real importance to the cultural life of Naples. Its versatile members had musical as well as literary talents, and on at least one occasion a comedy was staged with music.[32]

Included among the founders of the Accademia dei Sereni were Gian Domenico da Nola and a number of musicians who also doubled as actors: Giovan Leonardo Salernitano, Luigi Dentice, and Giulio Cesare Brancaccio. Even before joining the Sereni, they had been featured in the first comedy known to have been performed in Naples by local artists, *Gli ingannati*, mounted in 1545 by Ferrante Sanseverino, the prince of Salerno, at his palace in the *seggio* Nido. Since 1536 Sanseverino had been influential in promoting the theater in Naples and developing it to the level it had reached in other Italian cities.[33] His sponsorship of comedies was suspended briefly during exile in France between 1544 and 1545, but upon returning he renewed his efforts. Antonino Castaldo, a Neapolitan historian, left a description of Sanseverino's productions documenting the roles of all the participants:

> In the year 1545 many Neapolitan gentlemen performed comedy for their practice and for the amusement of the city. The director of this [enterprise] was Signor Giovan Francesco Muscettola, a literary man of ready and biting wit. And having selected the comedy *Gli ingannati*, a work by the Sienese Accademia degli Intronati, with the most beautiful apparatus of lights, costumes, and music, they staged it in the hall of the prince of Salerno's palace, where the proscenium was always ready for such purpose. . . . Dentice, Mariconda, and delle Palle played the servants with marvelous grace, and Brancaccio played the lover [Flaminio, a major role] quite well; Muscettola played the Spaniard Giglio [a soldier] wondrously; Fabrizio Dentice, Luigi's son, played

Pasquella [the meddling old servant] aptly; Villano was a noble and serious pedant; Ricoveri played the old fool just crazily; and Salernitano, the aged Virginio very gravely; a son of Signora Giovanna Palombo played Fabio in very good taste, and all the others spoke so suitably that Naples did not have to envy Siena for its actors. Zoppino, a famous and judicious musician of the time, was in charge of the music and also of the consort of instruments, wherefore the music was truly heavenly; especially Dentice with his falsetto and Brancaccio with his bass voice performed miracles. In the following year, 1546, another comedy was staged, a work by Mariconda [member of Sanseverino's household] called *La Filenia*, performed by almost all the same actors with excellent music [selected by Vincenzo da Venafro], which was a great success.[34]

Given a plentiful supply of musical talent, Zoppino and Venafro may have inserted many songs directly into the action to enhance the imbroglio of mistaken identities and the portrayals of deceit, hoodwinking, and jealousy that characterize the plots of *Gli ingannati* (The deceived) and *La Filenia*.[35] There is no record of what songs were selected, but since many *villanesche* center on the notion of amorous deception (*inganno amoroso*), they would certainly have provided realistic ornaments to these plots. By 1545 a substantial number of three-part *villanesche* were in circulation. The first book had been published in Naples in 1537, close enough in time to the imperial visit to be considered a retrospective collection of songs that had graced the comedies played for the emperor as well as a sign of Neapolitan pride in the popularity of a local genre.[36] In 1541 Nola published two books containing *villanesche* and *mascherate*, whose parodistic treatment of deceitful love suggests origin in the theatrical festivities of Shrovetide that proliferated during the emperor's sojourn. Between 1542 and 1544 it appears that no comedies were staged nor any *villanesche* published by Neapolitans. Then, with the rekindling of comedy performances in 1545–46, came a sudden increase in the number of *villanesca* books brought out by Neapolitan composers (seven books in all), defining a reciprocal relationship between the *villanesca* and comedy.

By the time Lasso arrived in Naples, the Sereni had folded and comedy performances had waned in the *seggio* Nido. Sanseverino sponsored his last comedy in 1548 and then moved to Salerno. (His activities came to an abrupt end in 1552 when he was declared an enemy of the crown and his possessions and title were confiscated.) The first generation of native composers had ceased publication, if not production, of *villanesche*. Nola and Cimello turned to the madrigal about 1545.[37] Di Maio became *maestro di cappella* of the Neapolitan church SS. Annunziata in 1548. Nothing is known about Fontana, but some of his *villanesche* enjoyed an extended reception through Lasso's four-part arrangements. These early *villanesca* composers may have been informally connected to the artistic coterie at Sanseverino's court and stimulated by his enthusiasm for local lyric genres. He is the only Neapolitan nobleman of the period known to have written dialect poems, and the fact that he performed *napolitane* in 1544 when he was in exile at the French court suggests that he made a habit of promoting their use as forms of lighthearted entertainment.[38]

While native composers were occupied with other matters, Lasso cultivated Neapolitan songs, especially those that evoked *inganno amoroso*, a favorite topos among aristocratic supporters of comedy. Lasso appears to have been the only composer living in Naples between 1549 and 1551 to arrange three-part *villanesche* for vocal quartet,[39] and he may have assimilated the Neapolitan style earlier during his sojourn in Milan. Books of three-part *villanesche* spread rapidly to northern cities and courts during the 1540s through imperial channels and Venetian music presses, and four-voice arrangements circulated widely as well.

The ruin of the house of Sanseverino and the suspension of support for comedy by no means signaled the end of an era of artistic prosperity in Naples. Musical recreation continued to flourish at soirées in the *seggi*, and aristocratic taste for comic genres was no doubt satisfied by Lasso's *villanesche*. Among the leading entertainers were the versatile noblemen from Sanseverino's troupe. They participated in both soloistic and polyphonic ensembles, a juxtaposition of media that was as common at informal gatherings as in the theater.[40] In his *Due dialoghi della musica* of 1552, Luigi Dentice described "una bella musica" he had heard at parties given by Giovanna d'Aragona, presumably dating from the time Lasso was in Naples.[41] Dentice named the musicians who routinely performed vocal chamber music together, a mixture of amateurs and professionals customary in Naples as elsewhere.[42] Among the instrumentalists were "M. Giovanleonardo dell'Arpa napoletano [the Abate Giovanleonardo Salernitano], M. Perino da Firenze, M. Battista Siciliano, and M. Giaches da Ferrara [Wert]." The singers were M. Scipione delle Palle and the noblemen Giulio Cesare Brancaccio and Francesco Bisballe (conte di Briatico), who also performed in the viceroy's chambers ca. 1550.

Giambattista Del Tufo, a Neapolitan patrician who recounted the marvels of his city, boasted that every Neapolitan was almost born singing and that ordinary citizens as well as nobles could "placate the anger and fury of every obstinate heart" ("placan l'ira, e 'l furore d'ogni ostinato core") with their songs.[43] With typical Neapolitan pride the academician Benedetto di Falco voiced the consequences of such pervasive innate talent: "Besides that natural instinct for music, with which it appears that heaven has en-dowed every Neapolitan, almost everyone adds art to nature; and day and night, sometimes with voices, sometimes with instruments, diverse harmonies of heavenly sweetness are heard in various locations."[44] The Neapolitan courtly milieu had fostered lyric styles of musical entertainment since the first generation of accomplished improvisers emerged in the late fifteenth century, led by Il Chariteo and the young Serafino Aquilano. The vogue for improvisatory singing intermingled with composed music as time went on. But equally valued in Naples were the orally transmitted dialect songs that migrated from the rural provinces and flourished in urban culture. By 1537 oral and written song traditions had converged in the *villanesca*. That *villanesca* composers self-consciously imitated the habits of untrained musicians is clear from Lodovico Zacconi's perceptive observations published at the end of the century and written with the advantage of historical hindsight (by this time the genre had acquired the designation *villanella*):

> It should not be considered improper if [there are successive parallel fifths] in songs that imitate airs invented by singers having no knowledge of music. . . . We see all kinds of people do this in trying to sing the same verse that is sung by another. They seek agreeable sounds and tones with which to render it like a written part-song. Therefore, we can believe that musicians, having observed such practices with the help of both ear and nature, have also given written *villanelle* this form, in which it can be seen that *villanelle* and other trifles are not simple airs but pertain to art music and are made according to the rules of music; yet being the kind of airs I have mentioned, they proceed in imitation of those unpolished airs.[45]

The key to understanding the genesis and reception of the *villanesca* lies in the social structure of Naples, a capital city in which the seignorial class, artisans, and servants had a long history of association, dependency, and familiarity with one another's customs and language. In particular the influx of workers from the rural provinces during the first half of the sixteenth century encouraged interaction between oral and written traditions. Fernand Braudel remarks that "peasants from throughout the provinces of the vast mountainous and pastoral Kingdom flocked into the city. They were attracted by the *arti* of wool and silk; by the city's public works begun in the time of Pietro di Toledo and carried on long after him; . . . by domestic employment in the households of nobles, for it was becoming the fashion for aristocrats to live in the city and display their wealth."[46] Between 1500 and 1550 the population had increased fivefold owing to Spanish rule, which brought in many families connected with the interests of Spain. There were 212,203 inhabitants at mid-century and 280,000 at the end (twice that of Venice and three times that of Rome).[47] By the time Lasso arrived on the scene, the *villanesca* was established as a form of urban popular music to be enjoyed by all social classes. In sophisticated courtly circles it functioned as the comic companion of the serious madrigal, but at a deliberately lower level as an evocative reflection of unwritten traditions.[48] Its barbed allusions were directed at character types familiar in southern Italian culture—courtesans, artisans, Spaniards, courtiers—whose human frailties were brought into focus with the intent to amuse in an incongruous mixture of dialectal proverbial lore and Petrarchist imagery. It is conceivable that Lasso's *villanesche* (and their Neapolitan models) were received in Naples as covert forms of protest against oppressive Spanish rule. *Villanesche* always project a vigorous Neapolitan identity whether the popular elements predominate or are lightly submerged. They would have exerted a strong appeal to a degenerating aristocracy struggling to save face under the iron rule of the Spanish viceroyalty, which drained the resources of the kingdom with unjust taxation and closed the doors of humanist academies.

In fall 1551 Lasso departed Naples for Rome, where for about six months he was a guest in the household of Antonio Altoviti, archbishop of Florence, who resided in Rome because of differences with the Medici. Lasso then served for about a biennium as *maestro di cappella* at St. John Lateran until spring 1554, when he left to visit his ailing parents in Mons.[49] Discovering that they had died before his arrival, Lasso was alone and without prospects of an official position. By Quickelberg's account he then journeyed first to England, then to France with Giulio Cesare Brancaccio, whom he had probably met in Naples.[50] Brancaccio was not only a singer and actor but also a professional soldier who was addicted to a life of risk and adventure and who served at various times in the armies of the emperor and the king of France. The real purpose of the trip to England cannot be satisfactorily documented, and any hope that Lasso may have had of finding work at the English court was defeated by the political intrigues in which Brancaccio was embroiled, leading to arrest and expulsion from the country in July 1554.[51] Lasso went to Antwerp, where he remained for two years. The cast of imperial players who had dominated his adolescence was large and the roles wonderfully varied—from the arrogant Ferrante Gonzaga to the wily Brancaccio, mediated by d'Azzia, the genial scholar. Having come full circle through Hapsburg domains during the emperor's twilight years, Lasso observed the balance of power shifting toward the maritime nations of western Europe, so he chose his new venue wisely. Affluent Antwerp offered him not only the continuity of imperial connections but also the patronage of merchant capitalists and the support of a music printer to launch his fledgling career as composer.

An "Opus I"

In 1555 the Flemish music printer Tielman Susato published the fourteenth and final book in a chanson series he had begun in 1543, shortly after settling in Antwerp. *Le quatoirsiesme livre* is a miscellaneous collection of Lasso's madrigals, *villanesche*, chansons, and motets.[52] Popularly termed Lasso's "Opus I," this miscellany not only signaled the young composer's northern debut in a manner consistent with his precocious versatility but also confirmed Susato's reputation as a master craftsman. *Le quatoirsiesme livre* stands quite apart from the other books in Susato's chanson series owing to the unusual set of circumstances surrounding its publication.[53] To accommodate Lasso's book—the first containing Italian music to be printed in the Low Countries—Susato willingly suspended his current projects. Then, fitting the unplanned book into his normal production scheme (traditionally organized by numbered series), he appended it to the first chanson series and formulated a special title, claiming that the contents were made "in the new manner of certain Italians" ("a la Nouvelle composition d'aucuns d'Italie").

Susato reissued Lasso's first opus within the year under an Italian title that designated the book as first in a series (see plate 2). Because *Il primo libro* contains a dedication, it has commonly been considered the first edition of Lasso's "Opus I," *Le quatoirsiesme livre* the reprint or second edition. However, *Il primo libro* is actually a second issue within the first edition, printed concurrently with *Le quatoirsiesme livre* from substantially the same setting of type.[54] The relationship between issues (and an intervening variant state) has been documented on the basis of patterns in the correction process.[55] There is good reason to believe that Lasso participated as corrector in the production of his "Opus I." Evidence of his intervention between issues is found in the remarkably accurate texts of *Il primo libro*, particularly with respect to underlay. Moreover, Lasso's help would have been a distinct advantage in proofing the Italian texts, for Susato had never printed Italian before.

Lasso's dedication in *Il primo libro* is addressed to Stefano Gentile, a Genoese merchant-banker and connoisseur of polyphonic music who resided in Antwerp.[56] It is possible that Gentile commissioned the Italian-titled issue of Lasso's "Opus I" expressly for the large community of Genoese merchants based in Antwerp.[57] The title page and dedication in Italian are unique among Susato's publications and provide compelling evidence for a marketing strategy oriented toward a particular audience. After Susato dis-

Illus. 2. Portrait of Lasso about age twenty-eight by Hans Mielich, from the Tenor partbook of *Prophetiae Sibyllarum*. Reproduced by permission of the Österreichische Nationalbibliothek, Vienna, MS. Mus. 18744.

tributed all the copies of the first edition, he brought out a second concealed edition dated 1555 but actually published about 1558.[58] A third and final edition came out in 1560. Both reprint editions contain numerous typesetting errors. They do not meet the high standard set by *Il primo libro*, which stands as positive proof of the relationship that evolved between a young composer and a master printer as they united expertise to uphold a high standard of artistry and craftsmanship.

Transmission of the "Opus I" Villanesche

International publication of the six *villanesche* in Lasso's "Opus I" began in 1565 when the Parisian firm of Le Roy and Ballard printed them for the first time outside the Low Countries. Between 1565 and 1629 they were repeatedly included in a wide variety of publications (vocal and instrumental and often in anthologies) issued by Le Roy and Ballard in Paris, Phalèse in Louvain and Antwerp, and Bernhard Jobin in Strasbourg (see table 1). The vogue for intabulations had run its course by 1584, when the last such arrangement of Lasso's Neapolitan songs appeared, but as vocal pieces these *villanesche* continued to circulate well into the seventeenth century due to the efforts of Phalèse the younger. As far as it is known, the *villanesche* were never printed in Italy, the Iberian peninsula, or England, although they were exported

to these countries through the book trade and circulated in manuscript copies. Their transmission will now be traced by geographical region with special attention to the contributions of printers, scribes, and intabulators. Juxtaposed in various collections with Lasso's chansons, these *villanesche* perhaps gained recognition by favorable comparison to a genre of wide popularity with the composer's patrons and publishers.

FRANCE

Le Roy and Ballard included the set of six *villanesche* in their collection titled *Dixhuictieme livre de chansons* (1565), placing these works in a central position between sets of four- and five-part chansons by Lasso and in the same order in which they appeared in "Opus I." Residual strophes for each piece were grouped at the bottom of the recto page, and, as in Susato's editions, refrain cues were omitted. When Le Roy and Ballard reprinted the *villanesche* in their extensive miscellany *Continuation du mellange d'Orlande de Lassus* (1584), they again situated them as a set in their original order but improved the readings by adding refrain cues. Le Roy and Ballard were the ones primarily responsible for promoting Lasso's music in France, beginning in 1559 with the publication of individual works in anthologies and expanding after 1564 to collections, among which are *Les meslanges d'Orlande de Lassus* and the first edition of *Libro de villanelle* (1581). These books attest to the strong friendship that developed between Lasso and Le Roy upon the composer's visits to Paris and helped to secure the firm's preeminence while increasing Lasso's international reputation.[59] Proof of the high regard felt for Lasso in France at this time is the author's *privilège* granted him by Charles IX in 1571, protecting all the works he had ever composed and printed in France as well as all future publications for a period of ten years.[60] All things considered, Le Roy was more partial to Lasso's chansons than to any other genre, selecting eleven of them as models for intabulation in his lute instruction book (1574). He never intabulated Lasso's *villanesche* or published them in his many tablature books. It was his counterpart in the Low Countries, Pierre Phalèse, who first captured that corner of the market.

LOW COUNTRIES

Throughout his career as music printer, Pierre Phalèse the elder (ca. 1510–ca. 1576) published an array of lute and cittern books that hold an important place in the annals of music printing. Phalèse was the first to publish intabulations of Lasso's works.[61] His son Pierre Phalèse the younger continued his father's association with Jean Bellère, begun in 1570. In 1581 he moved the business from Louvain to Antwerp, where he brought out one of his finest books, *Pratum Musicum* (1584) by the Antwerp lutenist Emanuel Adriansen. This volume contains two arrangements of Lasso's *Madonna mia, pietà*, one for three lutes and the other for lute and two voices. Phalèse the elder's *Theatrum Musicum* (1571) contains the most comprehensive collection of Lasso's *villanesche* ever intabu-

lated for solo lute (see table 2). The house of Phalèse also published intabulations of some *villanesche* for four-course cittern in the *Hortulus Cytharae* books of 1570 and 1582. The intabulator of Lasso's works in these collections is unknown, but it is presumed that the house employed one on a regular basis.[62]

As Lasso's publisher in the Low Countries after the Susato firm closed in 1564, Phalèse issued several books devoted to Lasso's vocal compositions, including many pieces never before published. When Lasso obtained author's privileges protecting his works in France and Germany, where the market was better and international circulation through the trade more secure, the house of Phalèse gradually lost its leading status and was eventually reduced to publishing reprint editions of his works. (A case in point is *Libro de villanelle* [1582].) Phalèse the elder published Lasso's *villanesche* in his *Second livre des chansons* (1570), an anthology shared with Rore and Monte. Lasso's *villanesche* stand first in the anthology, ordered as in Susato's fourteenth book. Phalèse claimed to have "newly edited and emended" the contents, and indeed his readings of the *villanesche* are remarkably accurate. There is no doubt that he used one of Susato's editions as copy text; the text underlay is identical and set, like Susato's, in a small italic typeface. Phalèse departed singularly from previous traditions by omitting the residual strophes, and his son perpetuated this economical arrangement when he reprinted the *villanesche* in *La fleur des chansons* (1592).

ENGLAND

About the same time that Lasso's *villanesche* attained wide circulation on the Continent, they reached England in manuscript partbooks dated 1564–66, believed to have been copied in the Low Countries, perhaps commissioned as a gift for Queen Elizabeth.[63] These so-called Winchester Partbooks (Winchester College, Warden and Fellows' Library, MS. 153) still bear their original covers tooled with the Tudor arms. Lasso's *villanesche* are located in the main corpus, which is divided into two parts. The first part contains eighty-one settings of Italian texts and the second sixteen French chansons (two by Lasso). The majority of compositions are Neapolitan songs dating from 1545 to 1560, including thirty-five by Lasso's Flemish contemporary Hubert Waelrant. It is not known if the decided preference for *villanesche* reflects the taste of the person who commissioned the manuscript or an enthusiastic response to Italian popular music at Elizabeth's court during the early years of her reign. The scribe probably used Susato's first edition of "Opus I" as his copy text for Lasso's *villanesche* because Susato's one substantive spelling error (corrected in his reprints) was replicated in all the partbooks of Winchester 153 ("forsse" instead of "fosse"

TABLE 2
Instrumental Arrangements of Lasso's "Opus I" *Villanesche*

	Novae eleg. cantilenae	*Renovata Cythara*	*Hortulus Cytharae*	*Theatrum Musicum*	*Toppel Cythar*	*Hortulus Citharae*	*Pratum Musicum*	CoimU 242
Brown no.	[1569]$_4$	[1569]$_5$	1570$_3$	1571$_6$	1575$_3$	1582$_5$	1584$_6$	ca. 1586
Reprint(s)	1574$_1$	[1575]$_2$ 1578$_4$ 1580$_2$	[1575]$_7$		1578$_5$			
Intabulator	Kargel	Kargel	anon.	Kargel	Kargel	anon.	Adriansen	anon.
Instrument	lute	four-course cittern	four-course cittern	lute	six-course cittern	four-course cittern	three lutes/ lute, S-B	keyboard
Tablature	Italian 0 = open string	Italian 0 = open string	French a = open string	French a = open string	Italian 0 = open string	French a = open string	French a = open string	keyboard partitura
Tuning	Gcfad'g'*	agd'e'†	bgd'e'†	Gcfad'g'†	BGdgd'e'*	agd'e'†	Adgbe'a'† Gcfad'g'† DGcead'†	
Fretting	chromatic	diatonic‡	chromatic	chromatic	chromatic	diatonic‡	chromatic	
La cortesia	x	x	x	x	x	x		x
Madonna mia	x	x	x	x	x	x	xx	
'No giorno								x
'Sto core mio		x	x	x		x		
Tu sai, madonna				x	x			
Tu traditora			x	x				

* Lowest line of tablature represents the highest course.
† Highest line of tablature represents the highest course.
‡ Whole tone between frets d and e.

in *'Sto core mio*). One *villanesca*, *'No giorno*, was omitted; otherwise the pieces appear in Susato's order.

GERMANY

Bernhard Jobin, music printer in Strasbourg from 1570 to ca. 1594, and his house intabulator, Sixt Kargel, were central figures in promoting instrumental arrangements of Lasso's music. Kargel was a lutenist of some renown, having served the landgrave of Alsace and Cardinal Charles of Lorraine in this capacity.[64] His contributions include original ornamented fantasias and dance pieces as well as intabulations of current French and Italian compositions, and his versatile talent satisfied the practical needs of both professional and amateur players, a fact reflected in title page notices promoting his intabulations as "easy to learn." *Toppel Cythar*, one of Kargel's and Jobin's most significant products, was published to meet the rising demand for music to play on the new fully chromatic cittern with six double-strung courses. Kargel boldly claimed the instrument as his own invention, although it had originated in Italy.[65] *Toppel Cythar* contains a varied repertory of compositions for Kargel's noble patrons including chansons and three *villanesche* by Lasso, following what was by then a well-established pattern of juxtaposition.

IBERIAN PENINSULA

The rapid exportation of music books throughout Europe owed much to the annual book fairs attended by sellers and collectors. Thus, it is not surprising to discover two of Lasso's *villanesche*—*La cortesia*, one of the most popular among intabulators, and *'No giorno*, which had not been intabulated elsewhere but which follows *La cortesia* in "Opus I"—in an Iberian keyboard manuscript (Coimbra, Biblioteca Geral da Universidade, MS. 242).[66] The manuscript, an extensive anthology of 230 compositions copied ca. 1586, is written throughout in open score with clefs disposed in descending order of range. The handwriting is lively and careless, resulting in inexact alignment of notes. Barlines, drawn by an unaided hand through each brace, mark off semibreves. The scribe evidently copied the *villanesche* from one of Susato's editions, probably the copy of *Le quatoirsiesme livre* (first issue) exported to Spain by the Antwerp bookseller Jan van der Loe in 1556.[67] His readings agree in significant detail with Susato's and show none of the variants in collections printed after 1565.

Villanesca *Traditions, 1537–55*

Following its debut in print in 1537, the *villanesca* developed along parallel lines in three-part settings by Neapolitan composers and four-part arrangements based on Neapolitan models. The three-part *villanesche* in this edition (Lasso's models) represent the Neapolitan line that extended to the north in 1541 when Nola's collected works were published by Scotto in Venice.[68] Overall Nola's *villanesche* were preferred as models by arrangers, although Fontana's were highly popular as well. Of Lasso's eighteen arrangements, five have models by Fontana and three by Nola.

The Neapolitan *villanesca* is a strophic song scored as a high-pitched vocal trio and is distinguished by stylistic elements rooted in oral traditions. The dominant melodic voice is the cantus, which proceeds in short, well-rounded strains, setting the poem line by line in irregular rhythmic patterns closely allied to word accents. Such popular tunes (or *arie*, to use the term then current) have been described as unfolding "with an immediacy that [gives] to their progress the sense of an inevitable course aimed at a precise goal."[69] The tune is supported by note-against-note counterpoint that occasionally gives way to short points of imitation at the unison or fifth. The tenor and bass parts, so-called, actually have ranges about a fifth higher than normal, and all three parts move within a narrow ambitus seldom exceeding two octaves. The tenor shadows the tune closely in parallel thirds except at cadences, when it normally creates a 4–3 suspension with the bass. Consecutive fifths disposed in close position were used discreetly by some composers, liberally by others, in cadential areas or in conjunct phrases (cf. nos. [10], [24], and [27]). The Neapolitan composer derived his habitual use of parallel motion from complementary models in popular culture, such as the self-accompanying singer who, in harmonizing *arie*, moved his hand in a fixed position along the fingerboard of a rudimentary stringed instrument. The other model, described by Zacconi, involves vocal improvisation of the harmonizing parts: "Those ignorant [of the rules] of music . . . do not care, since they do not know any better, about making two or more fifths. . . . Having hit upon such consonances, popular singers do not know any other way of moving to neighboring tones but have the feeling of being well accompanied."[70]

The traditional singing style in the southern Mediterranean area is high-pitched and strained. Thus, the Neapolitan composers' predilection for highly placed triadic sonorities suggests they sought to imitate a regional sound pattern. Most *villanesche* were conceived for two high voices and one lower one, according to their clef combinations. Also southern in origin is the breaking off of words and phrases, then resuming in a new melodic start.[71] The derivation of the tunes is more difficult to establish, although they are genetically related and contain stereotyped melodic formulas, especially at cadences. But the amount of personal variation suggests that for the most part Neapolitan composers imitated rather than quoted genuine tunes. They were careful, however, to preserve the descent by step to the tonic at line endings typical of Mediterranean (and pan-European) folk music.

The *villanesca* poem is essentially a *strambotto* (eight-line poem in symmetrical couplets) expanded to four strophes by the insertion of a refrain after each couplet: (1) *ab* + R, (2) *ab* + R, (3) *ab* + R, (4) *cc* + R or *ab* + R. The length of the refrain varies from poem to poem. The strophes are set to identical music and are characterized by repeating strains: AA B CC for the strophe consisting of a couplet and one refrain line (no. [9]); AA B C DD for a couplet and two refrain lines (no. [24]), and so on.[72] These standard types were subject to numerous variations, but with a decided preference for repeated strains at the beginning and end. Loose constructions in the grammar and syntax of *villanesca* poems re-create colloquial speech patterns. Proverbial sayings, regional metaphors, and euphemistic expressions, strung together with occasional pseudo-Petrarchan images, come to an epigrammatic close in the final couplet. In sum, the primary attraction of the Neapolitan *villanesca* was its reflection of popular lyrical traditions; the generic designation (from *villano* or peasant) draws attention to a natural, unrefined air that always predominates despite limitations imposed by the rules of counterpoint.

The first *villanesca* arranger was Adrian Willaert, who, objecting to the high-pitched vocal timbre of his Neapolitan models, moved the tune to the tenor part where he could harmonize it with balanced choral sonorities. The "whole process of rewriting the three-voice pieces of the Neapolitans into four-voice *villanesche*," according to Pirrotta, "was meant as an improvement, bringing back a pleasurable but unruly genre into the regularity of *ars musica*."[73] Willaert published only one book of *villanesche* (1544), but it circulated in four reprint editions between 1545 and 1553.[74] He established two basic approaches to arrangement, one literal and the other free, and both were readily adopted by other composers. In the literal arrangement there is extensive quotation of vertical cross sections from the model, a matter of inverting the positions of the cantus and tenor and retaining the bass line with minor modifications. Arrangers usually eliminated any stepwise root movement that had generated parallel fifths in the model, and they made chord substitutions when the original bass line was static or redundant. They quoted the Neapolitan tune rather literally to impress its salient features upon the new product, namely, the teasing truncations and irregular rhythmic patterns. However, they often led the final tone of each phrase upward to create a cadential chord with a raised third degree. In the free arrangement there is no inverted relationship between cantus and tenor, and the cantus is a melody with a distinctive profile, not merely a duplication of the tenor. Increased attention to the uppermost part usually generated extensive reharmonization of the tune. The tune itself was subject to a variety of treatments. It could be quoted intact phrase by phrase in the tenor, or it could become a *vagans*, migrating from part to part. Some composers preferred to leave it in the cantus. Free arrangements are characterized by juxtaposition of passages quoted literally from the model with reworked passages. Some free arrangements resemble parodies owing to the liberal insertion of new material and extensive motivic and rhythmic development. Often only the first phrase of the tune is quoted verbatim and subsequent phrases are either paraphrased or newly composed.

Lasso as Arranger

Lasso's *villanesca* arrangements were published in 1555 and 1581 at widely separated times in his career, but they stem from the journeyman period. The dedication in the *Libro de villanelle* (1581) supports an early date for its contents: "It would have been more appropriate had I published these *villanelle* in my youth when I composed them rather than now in my mature age. I was not enthusiastic about publishing them, but my friends were so insistent that I have been forced to observe their wishes rather than my better judgment."[75] Lasso's apologetic tone implies that he viewed his *villanelle* retrospectively as juvenilia, and it invites speculation that he may have revised some of them before publication. In the stylistic categorization that follows, I proceed on the assumption that Lasso's entire repertory of arrangements dates from ca. 1550 to 1555. Within each category I distinguish arrangements whose models can be traced from those whose models cannot. The latter were certainly based on lost compositions by Neapolitan composers or by Lasso himself because they contain tunes and texts in an unmistakable Neapolitan style. No attempt has been made to arrange the compositions in chronological order, but pieces that appear to be revisions or more mature in conception are noted.

LITERAL ARRANGEMENTS

Six compositions qualify as literal arrangements. Two are very strict in their appropriation of preexistent materials: [4] *'Sto core mio* (1555) and [16] *O occhi manza mia* (1581). They consist almost entirely of vertical cross sections from their anonymous models

(nos. [10] and [27], respectively), with the contratenor filling out the sonorities.[76] [1] *La cortesia* and [3] *'No giorno* (1555) are constructed along similar lines, but the inverted relationship between cantus and tenor is looser in some strains where modest reworking of the original textures occurs. (Cf. nos. [7] and [1], [9] and [3].) They are the only arrangements in which the stepwise descent of the tenor tune is preserved at all internal phrase endings. Two arrangements lacking traceable models complete this category: [22] *S'io ve dico* (1581) and [6] *Tu, traditora* (1555), both containing tunes that are unmistakably Neapolitan. The cantus of what was originally a three-part setting of *Tu, traditora* is extant in a Roman anthology bearing no internal attributions, but with Lasso's name in the title (*Villanelle d'Orlando di Lassus e d'altri eccellenti musici libro secondo* [Rome: V. Dorico, 1555]). Thus, Lasso's arrangement may have been based on his own setting left behind in Rome. (For a transcription of the cantus that Lasso quotes almost verbatim in the tenor of his arrangement, see commentary to no. [6].)

FREE ARRANGEMENTS

There are eight free arrangements in Lasso's repertory, two with traceable models and six without. In [2] *Madonna mia, pietà* and [5] *Tu sai, madonna* (both from 1555), the tune is quoted intact in the tenor, and a highly expressive cantus part is added. (For the respective models, see nos. [8] and [11].) The melodic contours of the cantus in *Madonna mia, pietà* expand and contract to depict the erotic fantasies of a frustrated lover, a madrigalian touch that was no doubt responsible for the work's great popularity. *Tu sai, madonna* is Lasso's only arrangement in which homophonic textures are enlivened by melismas. The six free arrangements without traceable models are all located in *Libro de villanelle*. Four of these—[14] *Io ti voria*, [17] *Ogni giorno*, [20] *S'io fusse ciaul'*, and [21] *S'io ti vedess'una sol*—form a subgroup in the total repertory because their tunes, which are clearly Neapolitan, migrate. In these arrangements melodic formulas at phrase endings determine the part in which the tune is located. Some recurrent formulas are (by scale degree) 4–3–4–2–1 (or 3), 5–3–4–2–1 (or 3), or a scalar descent from the fourth or fifth degree to the root or third. More advanced in conception are [23] *Tutto lo dì* and [18] *Par ch'hai lasciato*, which have affinities with *Madonna mia, pietà* and *Tu sai, madonna* because the tunes, intact in the tenor, inspired cantus parts with effective changes of register and contour to accommodate the meaning of the text. The cantus of *Par ch'hai lasciato* has a much higher range than the cantus in any other arrangement, and this setting is unique in its use of melodic chromatic motion. Its musical form is also unusual, for the couplets are varied from strophe to strophe. These singular qualities suggest that *Par ch'hai lasciato* was composed or revised to meet the requirements of a special occasion, of which more will be said later.

Parodies

Four arrangements—[12] *Ad altre le voi dare*, [13] *Ecco la nimph'Ebrayca*, [15] *O belle, fusa!* and [19] *Saccio 'na cosa* (all from *Libro de villanelle*)—quote the first phrase of the model tune verbatim (or nearly so) in the tenor voice, then proceed more freely, dwelling on rhythmic-declamatory features of the model and exaggerating its Neapolitan mannerisms in one way or another. (For Lasso's models, see nos. [24], [25], [26], and [28], respectively.) *O belle, fusa!* for example, is notable for the stuttering effect attained in the refrain by truncation of the suggestive word "fusa," which received no particular attention in the model. This is the only arrangement besides [18] *Par ch'hai lasciato* in which single words are broken off. Lasso's droll sense of humor is most evident in his refrains, where he vigorously animates the original patter declamation to bring forward witty wordplay.

To summarize, two quite different compositional processes underlie Lasso's approach to arranging. In one the arrangement is structurally dependent upon the older composition; in the other the borrowed material is more freely developed, often but not always with reference to the overall structure of the model and sometimes only by allusion to its beginning. A characteristic feature of his so-called *villanella* style[77] is the pervasive, lively, homorhythmic texture that ensures maximum intelligibility of the text, an approach far removed from that favored by arrangers in Willaert's circle who could not repress the urge to gloss their models contrapuntally. Lasso, whose imagination was stimulated by popular traditions, preferred to convert any imitative textures in his models to homophony. His arrangements contain many progressions in which the bass moves by a major or minor third up or down to create cross relations. Equally characteristic are chains of progressions with the bass moving by fifths or fourths to establish temporary departures from the mode. The use of root-position chords colored by accidentals (and not always textually determined) was common among Italian madrigalists at mid-century and not restricted to any one locality.[78] Lasso's cultivation of "diatonic" chromaticism was thus in keeping with a general trend. Thirteen of his arrangements are in the Dorian mode on D or G (determined by the tune's structure), but he often undermined this mode by adding or removing accidentals in the tune and emphasizing dissonant modal degrees at structurally significant points.

Reception History

Italy

By 1555 the *villanesca* was in place in humanist circles as a cheerful complement to the serious love poem in which feminine fidelity and physical perfection were traits to be idealized or overcome by persuasive male rhetoric. In *villanesca* poetry feminine deceit and masculine frustration control a love-hate relationship, disordering it without resolution, both genders bearing the brunt of chauvinistic jests—the cheated and the cheat caught up in the web of illicit, treacherous love. *Villanesca* poets, most of whom were also composers, pursued two styles: a low style in dialect or city vernacular and a "higher" style with a greater incidence of pseudo-Petrarchan expressions and a milder tone. The latter gradually ascended in popularity after about 1560 and acquired the gentler genre designation *villanella*. Most poems among Lasso's settings are in the low style, pointing both to a personal predilection and to the taste of his supporters in Naples and Rome. Only three poems can be described as mildly Petrarchan (nos. [4], [21], and [22]). In the low style there is a subtype narrated by a gullible suitor puffed with rage and frustration, having been duped by a scheming, traitorous woman. His masculine pride is so sorely wounded that he is reduced to making abusive assaults on her character (nos. [3], [12], [13], [17], [18], and [23]). The remaining low-style poems are less vindictive and consist mainly of erotic allusions or frank pleas for relief from cruel teasing (nos. [1], [2], [5], [6], [14], [15], [16], [19], and [20]). Most of these could be described as playful serenades in which the lover harps on the theme of his martyrdom; no. [15], however, is a licentious masking song, and no. [19] is an erotic riddle.

The *villanesca* poems in Lasso's repertory concern illicit affairs in which the love object is a courtesan or, in at least one case, a common prostitute (no. [13]). Italian aristocrats had plenty of experience with these women, for they apparently took up the Spanish custom of frequenting their circles.[79] In Naples, Rome, and Venice, where *villanesche* thrived, prostitution was a major industry. The profession of courtesan, more closely resembling the Greek hetaera than harlot, had its earliest flowering in Rome and spread quickly to other cities where it was considered an acceptable outlet among cultured men and a preserver of marriage. Common property in Venice during the 1550s was a list of the "principal and most illustrious courtesans," including their addresses and fees.[80] *Villanesca* poets exploited the lowlife of the demimonde for comical reasons, because the wily tactics of courtesans were taken for granted in a society that regarded "all but the greatest of them almost as pretty toys, but ones which could easily be broken and thrown away."[81] Satirists centered on the consequences of tangling with such women. The following portrait of a Neapolitan courtesan, drawn by Giambattista Basile in his eclogue "The Crucible," provides a perspective for the shrewd raillery in many *villanesche:*

> put her to the test
> And what a smoke you'll see—So many traps,
> Pitfalls and nets and snares and tangled skeins,
> For women will prepare a thousand plots,
> Invent a thousand wiles and stratagems,
> A thousand machinations they will plan,
> Ambushes, mines and later counter mines,
> Intrigues, entanglements. You will be drawn
> As by a hook: she'll bleed you barber-like
> And like a gypsy cheat you right and left.
> A thousand times you'll think that she is wine
> That sparkles, while she is but poisonous flesh.
> If she but speak, she plots—or if she move
> She'll weave a plan. E'en laughing she intrigues,
> And if she touches you she'll leave a stain.[82]

Courtesans were instructed in the arts and tricks of the profession by their mothers or by a *ruffiana* who also procured their clients. The *ruffiana* was an expert beautician who could hide the defects of age, concoct dyes to bleach hair to the fashionable gold, and mix waters to make the skin appear white, fresh, and virginal, a subterfuge that was an added attraction in bargaining (see no. [27] for a sensuous description of a young courtesan's attributes). From their crafty mentors courtesans learned to dress in a lascivious fashion, to devise love potions, to discourse on varied subjects, and to develop musical skills. "Anyone of them who had not learned a repertory of the most beautiful and recent *canzoni* would have been ashamed of herself."[83] Gallants who sought the company of courtesans would often send a *mezzano* with songs and love letters to aid in negotiating a meeting. This intermediary brought the latest madrigal or Neapolitan song to perform to his own accompaniment on the lute or viola da braccio. In sum, Neapolitan songs were sung directly to courtesans as forms of procurement or else by them as overt forms of seduction. Of the many accounts that confirm the role of Neapolitan songs in the demimonde, one dated 1546 is especially pertinent. A Roman gentleman, having spent his first night ever with a courtesan—a certain rising star from Naples—found her simply divine. They remained "happily alone together all the next day, dining in his house and singing Neapolitan songs."[84]

The archetypal courtesans of Lasso's time were Nanna and her daughter Pippa, fictitious creations of Pietro Aretino in his widely read *Ragionamenti,* two volumes of scurrilous dialogues (1534, 1536) marked by vivid, honest realism. There is a common denom-

Illus. 3. Venetian courtesan. Woodcut by Cesare Vecellio, *Habiti antichi et moderni di tutto il mondo* (Venice: Giovanni Bernardo Sessa, 1598), no. 111. Reproduced by permission of Dover Pictorial Archive Series.

inator between Aretino's *Ragionamenti* and many Neapolitan songs of the period, because "their speech is real speech [with] the cadence, the vocabulary, the sound and the taste of the language of tough people of his day."[85] Aretino's advice to writers even reads like a textbook for *villanesca* poets: "Use the language of your contemporaries; the customs of your day and age; the flavor of the world you live in. Above all, have something to say; something based on the fantastic mixture of farce and tragedy that swirls around you."[86] In *villanesca* poems the threats and complaints of male suitors derive from the real frauds perpetrated by courtesans. Lasso's audiences knew them well, for they are made notorious by Aretino's Nanna: "how to lure on the timid; how to keep a lover when you have him; how to play one lover against another; how to use vanity, jealousy, curiosity and every other weakness to which poor mortals, especially when male, are subject."[87]

While in Munich, Lasso evidently allowed manuscript copies of his dialect songs to circulate within the family of his patron, Duke Albrecht V, who ruled from 1550 to 1579. In a letter of 20 June 1574 to her brother the crown prince Wilhelm V, Archduchess Maria von Steiermark requested some of "Orlando's *villanesche* and *moresche*" because her husband enjoyed them; she wrote to Wilhelm again on 10 April 1577 to ask for more.[88] It is reasonable to suppose, then, that there were many occasions when Lasso's Neapolitan songs functioned as amusement pieces in Vienna (where the Steiermarks resided), at the Munich court, and at Trausnitz castle in Landshut (where Wilhelm lived from 1568 to 1579).

Massimo Troiano, a Neapolitan composer and alto in the Munich Kapelle from 1568 to 1570, was commissioned by Duke Albrecht to write an account of Wilhelm's wedding in 1568, a chronicle that would also magnify the splendor of Albrecht's court and musical establishment. Troiano's *Dialoghi* contains a valuable record of the kinds of music Lasso and his Kapelle furnished for daily recreation. Ducal meals, for example, were occasions for festive entertainment pieces; French chansons and "other cheerful works" were played on instruments between the first and second courses, madrigals and motets added to the fare later. At the fruit course, Troiano notes, "Messer Orlando di Lasso gives his singers free rein, and with sweet and clear voices they make everyone listen to compositions that are presented anew each day. And frequently, not without great satisfaction to the duke, expert and select singers render beautiful quartets and artful trios, so that I can attest to having seen His Excellency leave the table to listen to the harmony."[89] The "trios" Troiano refers to may have been published in a miscellany now lost: *Musica nuova dove si contengono madrigali, sonetti, villanelle et altri compositioni d'Orlando di Lasso a tre voci novamente da esso composte.* This book was listed frequently in fair catalogues and booktrade lists as having been published in Munich by the official court printer, Adam Berg, in 1594 or 1595.[90] Since the Italian title is unique in Berg's annals for Lasso, the miscellany could have been a reprint of an older edition published initially in Italy. Moreover, it may have contained *villanelle* that Lasso arranged and published in *Libro de villanelle.*

Troiano's *Dialoghi* features a detailed description of an improvised Italian comedy that he, Lasso, and other Italians in the Kapelle staged on a day's notice: [On Sunday morning, 7 March 1568,] "Duke Wilhelm of Bavaria had a whim to hear a comedy on the following day, and he sent for Orlando Lasso, who knew how to put anything into action. In the antechamber by chance Lasso found Troiano, who invented the plot, and between them they arranged the words."[91] With such versatile talent in attendance, this was probably not the first occasion on which Wilhelm indulged his taste for Italian comedy, nor was it to be the last. In the early 1570s professional comedians were employed at Trausnitz castle in Landshut. When Lasso went to Italy in 1574, he recruited more comic actors as well as musicians for Wilhelm. Faced with a mounting debt in 1575, Wilhelm had to dismiss his comedians, but in the following year, "he afforded himself the consolation of having the walls of the castle of Trausnitz frescoed with Pantaloons and Zanni. The narrow frieze to the ceiling of his bedchamber is alive with buffoons, banqueting, boating, serenading, and delivering love-letters; and the spiral staircase [in the Italian wing] painted with the same figures life-size is known as the Narrentreppe [Fools' Staircase]."[92]

During the interval of heightened enthusiasm for improvised Italian comedy, it would have been fitting for Lasso to draw upon his repertory for dialect songs that evoked the mask of Pantalone, the old Venetian merchant whose antics clearly amused the prince—Pantalone is depicted fifteen times in the Fools' Staircase. When in the throes of love, Pantalone typically vented the anger and complaints of old age, his comic attributes arising from the contradictions inherent in senility. Many of Lasso's Neapolitan songs can be associated with this persona, even though the texts are not in the Venetian dialect Pantalone spoke in his stage role. The gullible old lover was not restricted to Venice as his native city or place of residence at this date. Lasso himself played Pantalone in the 1568 comedy, a role with which he probably had some previous experience since it required baffling feats of agility and ridiculous backfalls. In the opening scene he introduced his character by singing two strophes of the famous *napolitana, Chi passa per 'sta strada*:

> From the other side of the stage appeared Messer Orlando dressed as a Magnifico in a crimson satin tunic, Venetian hose of scarlet, a long black mantle reaching to the ground and a mask that drew roars of laughter at first sight.
>
> He was playing a lute and singing: "Whoever passes down this street, and sighs not, happy man is he," and after repeating this twice he left the lute and began to complain of love, saying: "O poor Pantalone, you cannot go down this street without filling the air with sighs and watering the ground with tears."[93]

Troiano noted that between the second and third acts a song was rendered by "four voices, two lutes, a plucked string instrument, and a bass viol da gamba." A likely candidate for this song would be Lasso's *Par ch'hai lasciato*.[94] Its refrain refers to a certain Don Diego who, in the context of the comedy, would have been perceived as the swaggering Spanish captain, Don Diego di Mendozza, a role Troiano created for himself. By the end of the second act, the audience had heard the vain Don Diego boast of his acts of bravado and confess that a mere woman, the courtesan Camilla, had stolen his valiant heart. She in turn had coaxed a necklace from him by flattery and agreed to entertain him that evening. The action in the plot revolves around her cunning deceptions: she is maintained by Polidoro, but when he leaves town, she toys with Pantalone, the servant Zanni, and the Spaniard, whom she plants to make the other three jealous. In the third act she treats Don Diego (and Polidoro, who returns unexpectedly) to a stand-up, provoking a hilarious skirmish among all her suitors. Successful courtesans like Camilla managed their affairs cleverly so they could entertain other men besides their regular clients. But they were expected to obtain permission beforehand or suffer the consequences if caught in a clandestine rendezvous. The stand-up is a classic trick alluded to in several of Lasso's songs (nos. [3], [14], and [17]). But [18] *Par ch'hai lasciato* sets an explicit scene in which the cuckolded lover—who would speak for all of Camilla's suitors—even accuses the perpetrator of having taken on the arrogant manner of the Spaniard she has planted, for he knows the identity of his rival.

Lasso reinforces every innuendo of meaning in his setting, revealing the keen sense of timing and gesture upon which comedians rely. The opening couplet is declaimed in brisk rhythms that contrast with the broadened motion at the beginning of the refrain. Ironic chromaticism in the prolonged phrase "Deh, poverella" unwinds in mocking patter declamation only to slow down again in progressively retarded repetitions of "lo Don Diego." Drawing attention to the Spaniard's name in this droll manner exposes his weakness for courtesans and insinuates he will get what he deserves for his gullibility. The second strophe opens with a tantalizing truncation and proceeds in the same manner as the first. Musical jests accumulate in the couplet of the third strophe, where highly contrasting rhythmic patterns can be perceived as realistic imitations of mimed gestures. The chords on "tira" (go away) graphically point the way out, then boil up in accelerated declamation, advancing decisively through a circle of fifths to the flat side only to halt abruptly. After a gasp for breath the phrase plunges forward, stopping just in time for a fleeting chromatic progression on "vergognare." All the while the cantus pushes upward to its highest point, which, when attained, breaks off the word "giorno." This breathless activity continues through the final strophe, where juxtapositions of colorful harmonies and stuttering truncations accumulate in rapid succession.

In its vivid comical effects, *Par ch'hai lasciato* is closely allied to the "moresche, et altre canzoni" Lasso added to fill out the *Libro de villanelle* and that appear to date from the time comedy flourished at Munich and Landshut. The six-voice *moresche* had certainly been composed by 1568 because Troiano mentions they were performed by "six flutes and as many resonant voices" after a card game.[95] The weeks surrounding Wilhelm's marriage included many informal gatherings of family members, and it was probably on such occasions that the Steiermarks first heard the dialect songs they admired. But the fact that Archduchess Maria wrote to Wilhelm and not Albrecht for copies is proof that the songs also circulated at Landshut, where they functioned as evocative reminders of the quips and sallies of Italian comedians—all the more so after support for improvised comedy declined. Wilhelm, an ardent music lover and Lasso's friend since childhood, maintained a small branch of the main Kapelle at Landshut, also under Lasso's supervision.[96] Through letters (one signed "Orlando magnifique") and Lasso's periodic visits to Landshut (his wife's home town), Wilhelm and Lasso maintained close personal contact from the time of the marriage until Wilhelm returned to Munich. Wilhelm, then, was the conduit through which Lasso's dialect songs passed to a coterie of enthusiastic connoisseurs.

Performance Practice

During Lasso's lifetime ad hoc practices of arranging secular vocal music for instruments or mixed ensembles of voices and instruments flourished throughout Europe in theaters, academies, courts, private homes, and open-air spaces.[97] Interchangeability of performance media for a considerable corpus of vocal music was encouraged in book titles by the phrase "apt for voices and instruments." Similarly, almost all authors of embellishment manuals for singers maintained that their examples were also intended for "any kind of instrument."[98] Even though an increasing amount of music was being composed specifically for instruments, most of the instrumental repertory consisted of embellished intabulations of vocal polyphony that could be played as solos or accompaniments. Indeed, Lasso's widespread fame owed much to the fact that his secular compositions found favor among intabulators in the North and South.

Instrumental arrangements of Lasso's vocal compositions preserve performance traditions in written form that were normally not written down, such as the number and types of ornaments added by sixteenth-century musicians and *musica ficta*.[99] Consequently, intabulations are valuable resources for modern performers inclined to explore alternatives to the unembellished *a cappella* style that has prevailed in the performance of Lasso's secular music. The instrumentation and embellishment of vocal polyphony was, as Howard Mayer Brown has noted, often the preference of Renaissance musicians; moreover, "It is not easy to achieve a balanced, blended sound with a small group of solo singers without instrumental accompaniment; that it was no easier in the sixteenth century than it is today is suggested by the caution with which musicians then approached the task."[100] Lasso's Kapelle at Munich contained choice singers whose blend and impeccable intonation set a high standard, clearly a rarity in its time: "The sound from these controlled voices was so well united that the best ears could not distinguish one from another."[101] Yet this same Kapelle had in its ranks an array of instrumentalists who frequently played Lasso's music in mixed and pure consorts on occasions ranging from grand and solemn to intimate and informal.[102]

Ad hoc Arranging

Renaissance performers actively collaborated in the compositional process as ad hoc arrangers, exercising their prerogatives in selecting the medium, often with the guidance of a director like Lasso charged with organizing a musical event. Artistic choice was, of course, conditioned by the social setting, for example, the available space, the resources at hand, the talent of individual performers, and the idiosyncrasies of instruments. Players of chord-producing instruments were accustomed to reducing vocal polyphony to a form suitable for solo or accompaniment. As members of an ensemble they provided harmonic support on the so-called foundation instruments: lute, cittern, vihuela, guitar, and keyboards. If a desired composition was not available in an appropriate notation, the foundation player had to score or intabulate it. Evidence that players of fretted instruments could prepare their own intabulations is found in many instruction books that systematically detail the process of converting mensural notation to tablature, providing rules for strict literal reduction as well as models for ornamentation. Instrumentalists used the same embellishment techniques employed by singers and were encouraged to imitate the melodic flexibility of a trained voice.

Many amateur players of fretted instruments could not read staff notation and were unable to make their own reductions. They relied on music publishers to supply them with scores in tablature notation. Some European printers, among them Phalèse and Jobin, employed "editors" for the sole purpose of creating arrangements. The practical bent of Jobin's enterprise is revealed on the title page of his cittern anthology *Toppel Cythar* (1575), which contains some of Lasso's *villanesche*: "[These intabulations are] just as attractive in combination with other instruments as they are solo pieces in their own right" ("baides für sich selbs volkommenlich, und auch zu andern Instrumenten dinstlich zuspilen und zugebrauchen").[103] Cittern intabulations of Lasso's *villanesche* outnumber lute intabulations (see table 2), in keeping with the increased attention accorded the cittern in northern Europe during the 1570s when, according to Paolo Virchi, it gained acceptance among noble amateurs: "The citthara [cittern] has always stood in some consideration . . . because it . . . differs little from such instruments as the lute and the harpsichord, which have already attained perfection. But it is only now that the citthara begins to delight such noble personages as the Duke of Bavaria and Archduke Ferdinand of the Tyrol."[104] At the Bavarian court the cittern was often played in combination with a keyboard and flute.[105]

The tradition of instrumentation that has been documented most fully concerns Italian vocal music performed in theatrical contexts. This music tends to be homophonic and apt for large mixed ensembles. Until 1565 one or more chordal instruments supplied the harmony and blended the diverse colors of highlighting melodic instruments—from the same or different families—that doubled the outer parts. By 1589 the consort principle had been modified and extended in every way that the desire for variety could achieve, with individual instruments separated from their families.[106] Evidence regarding the performance of vocal music in chamber settings suggests that the same principles of instrumentation were applied here as well, but more discreetly according to spatial requirements. At its peak in 1568, Lasso's instrumental ensemble consisted of eight strings, seven winds, one lute, and two keyboards, but it often rendered Italian compositions in consorts of small proportions.[107]

Arranging Lasso's Villanesche

Since the *villanesche* in Lasso's "Opus I" remained in circulation throughout the sixteenth century, they were subject to a wide latitude of responses in respect to instrumentation, embellishment, and *musica ficta* as performance conventions changed. Many sourcebooks, manuals, and specialized studies provide useful criteria and alternatives for reconstructing these practices.[108] The guidelines given here are restricted primarily to performance traditions latent in the intabulations of Lasso's *villanesche* dating from 1570 to 1584. One composition, [2] *Madonna mia, pietà*, will serve as a case in point. It is a setting of a multi-strophic poem that adapts easily to what might be termed "suite" arrangement. The strophes are extended in length because of internal repetition, and thus an *a cappella* rendition of all strophes could be monotonous. Two effective options would be alternating strophes in *a cappella* and mixed consorts or reducing one or more strophes to solo and accompaniment.[109] If a program does not allow for protracted length, then one or two strophes can be omitted, but these should always be middle strophes, never the last.

The rich vertical sonorities and colorful false relations in *Madonna mia, pietà* are effectively reinforced by one or more foundation instruments. A variety of reductions for lute (nos. [30]–[32]) and for four-course and six-course cittern (nos. [37]–[38] and [42], respectively) are available in this edition for foundation function. Each intabulation is lightly ornamented, so some heterophony will result when the player is embellishing a line being sung as written. But this practice was tolerated and even encouraged in Lasso's time.[110] Number [30] for lute can be utilized without much modification of accidentals, since the intabulator followed the same conventions observed by singers in applying accidentals. There is one difference that requires an easy adjustment. In m. 32, Tenor, note 4, the intabulator changed Lasso's b♭ to a, which the lutenist can simply omit. Renaissance players of fretted instruments regularly accompanied singers and were accustomed to fitting their parts to the music being sung, generally conforming unless limitations of the instrument contravened. The cittern intabulations require more cooperation from the player because many of Lasso's original harmonies were altered to avoid difficult or impossible hand positions or to accommodate strumming. (Since the cittern is played with a quill plectrum, pitches have to be scored on adjacent strings.)

One passage in *Madonna mia, pietà* (mm. 15–20) shows consensus among all the intabulators regarding *musica ficta*. In m. 16, f' is raised in the uppermost voice despite the fact that it produces a forbidden interval (f♯' to b♭') and a false relation in m. 17 (see also mm. 18–19). This melodic progression reinforces the pathetic cry in the text, "Io grido e nol sentete," although it was probably not Lasso's original intention, or he would have marked it.[111] But since the progression became an acceptable performance tradition, I have incorporated the intabulators' accidentals as *musica ficta* in the vocal score. (These accidentals are, of course, optional in an *a cappella* performance.) Two arrangements of *Madonna mia, pietà* by Adriansen (nos. [31] and [32]) present another op-

tion in the application of *musica ficta*. In both of them f♯' appears on the second half of beat 2 in m. 16, but not in m. 18.

The broadened motion that sets off the phrase "Io grido" calls for ornamentation, and all the intabulators provided running figuration here, some more elaborate than others. Singers will discover that these instrumental *passaggi* can easily be transferred to the voice. Moreover, there are various other embellished passages, especially at cadences, that can be appropriated literally or adapted to suit a singer's range and ability. All the intabulators preferred to heighten the expressive contours of Lasso's superius with evenly flowing passagework reminiscent of the mid-century style. Singers learning the art of ornamentation will find these intabulations a convenient source for manageable *passaggi* and stereotypical graces. Embellishment in ensemble performance, as noted in instruction books, should not be too elaborate but largely restricted to cadences and evenly distributed among the parts. Solo vocal improvisation over chordal accompaniment allows for even more variety in embellishment, as does the reverse, when the accompanist ornaments and the singer adheres to the written part. Lasso's *Madonna mia, pietà* contains two melodic parts that can be extracted and sung by a soloist: the superius and the tenor (the latter has the original Neapolitan tune). The graceful ornamented line from the canto lute part in Adriansen's arrangement for three lutes (no. [31]) is effective when transferred to a high voice for soloistic rendition; the alto lute part would be a fitting choice for accompaniment.[112]

The flexible habits of Renaissance musicians are reflected in the format of Adriansen's collection *Pratum Musicum*: two or more voices of a vocal model facing a lute intabulation that can be played as a solo or an accompaniment.[113] Adriansen's intabulation of *Madonna mia, pietà* is a very strict transcription of all four polyphonic parts, ostensibly to provide the strongest possible harmonic support for playing in ensemble. But the thick chords often require full stops and advanced hand positions that are technically demanding. Both of Adriansen's arrangements of *Madonna mia, pietà* are attractive as they stand, yet they also accommodate other combinations. For example, a flute and viol could play (or double) the superius and bass parts in the vocal arrangement, and a keyboard player could take the difficult lute part. Likewise, in the arrangement for three lutes, the bass part (which doubles the vocal bass line an octave below) could be played on a keyboard, especially in large mixed ensembles where a thickened bass would balance and give depth to bright highlighting instruments. Combinations designed for halls of moderate proportions are quite effective if the outer parts are doubled at the octave above and below. For instance, in a mixed ensemble of transverse flute (or recorder), lute, harpsichord, bass gamba, and voices, the flute could double the superius at the octave above and embellish with the singer to expose the dominant melodic part further. The lute would provide support for the inner voices, while the harpsichord and gamba would unite to provide a sturdy doubled bass. The keyboard transcriptions placed parallel to the original tablature in this edition increase the options available to modern ensembles in making arrangements and accommodate groups who have no players of fretted instruments. Uniting keyboard scores with intabulations should encourage revival of the Renaissance practice of using fretted and keyboard instruments together in foundation roles. In selecting an appropriate keyboard instrument, modern players have a number of feasible choices: portative organ, virginal, spinet, and harpsichord.[114] The sonorities of the keyboard, however, should not overpower the fretted instrument if used in combination.

Some brief remarks about other *villanesche* in "Opus I" are necessary to resolve issues that might arise in arranging them. The instrumental sources of [4] *'Sto core mio*, for example, present a convenient alternative for transposition. Lasso scored it in a combination of high clefs (G2, C2, C3, and F3) with one flat in the signature, which means it can be transposed down a fourth if more comfortable for the voices.[115] Kargel brought this high-clef composition to the level of normal clefs in his lute intabulation, presumably to avoid using higher frets (see no. [33]). It should be noted that there are so many harmonic discrepancies between the cittern intabulations in Phalèse's *Hortulus Cytharae* (1570 and 1582) and their models that any attempt to use them as accompaniments would be impractical. A prime example is *Tu traditore* (no. [40]), which has also been transposed up a whole tone. A comparison of *Madonna mia pietà* in *Hortulus Cytharae* and in Kargel's *Renovata Cythara* (nos. [37] and [38], respectively) reveals many differences that derive from limitations posed by the instruments in question. The *villanesche* in *Renovata Cythara* were intabulated for a cittern tuned with a whole tone between the third and fourth courses. Kargel often chose to double tones either at the unison or octave, using the open a-string (French tuning). Phalèse's intabulator had a chromatically fretted cittern in mind (Italian tuning) and a preference for major sonorities scored as barred chords (see m. 3, chords 3 and 4). This expedient was not possible on Kargel's cittern.

In conclusion, it should be emphasized that descriptions of *villanesca* performances in Lasso's time are rare, but the ones that survive point to solo performance with lute accompaniment as the favored medium. This is consistent with both the great popularity of the instrument and the large numbers of *villanesche* intabulated for lute throughout the sixteenth century, some with superius in mensural notation.[116] Consideration should also be given to documentation that supports the performance of dialect songs in related genres (e.g., *villotte* and *moresche*) by pure consorts of voices or instruments of the same family.[117] Finally, it should be noted that Lasso's *villanelle* were probably performed *a cappella* at Landshut. Wilhelm's resources were quite limited, and between 1568 and 1570 the only instrumentalist was an organist. Wilhelm actively sought chamber players after that time, but court records suggest that he never acquired enough for varied consorts, although he always had a full complement of singers, including boys.[118]

Editorial Methods

Vocal Compositions

In this edition vocal compositions have been transcribed from first or second editions with all part-books intact. Variants between the main source and any relevant reprint editions are reported in the commentary under the headings "Notes on the Text" and "Notes on the Music." Texts are printed separately at the beginning of each critical report, and criteria used in text editing are summarized in the introduction to Texts, Translations, and Commentary. The compositions have been transcribed at original pitch and in their original note values. The incipit of each part includes the original clef, key signature, mensuration sign, and initial note (omitting any rests).

The mensuration sign in all main sources is C (*misura breve*) in contrast to the more typical ¢ (*misura commune*) of the period. The sign C was used regularly at mid-century for *villanesche* and for *note nere* (black-note) madrigals sharing the same scale of note values, with much of the text declaimed in minims and semiminims. French printers who published *villanesche* from Lasso's "Opus I" used the sign ¢, perhaps to suggest that the tempo should or could be quickened somewhat.[119] Editorial tempo markings have not been added to the transcriptions, but performers might consider Nicola Vicentino's observation that "*napolitane* demand a fast tempo from the start,"[120] the mensuration sign notwithstanding. For many compositions in this edition, the best choice for the tactus is the minim (half note). This unit of time beating was recommended by the Neapolitan composer and theorist Tomaso Cimello for compositions under the sign C moving mainly in smaller note values.[121]

Four *villanesche* contain passages with rhythmic patterns arranged in ternary groups of minims: no. [3] and its model no. [9], no. [20], and no. [23]. The notation varies from piece to piece, but in all cases minor sesquialtera proportion is a viable interpretation (three minims in the time of two). In nos. [3], [9], and [23] note values are blackened signifying a 3:2 relation. Number [23] lacks a signature; the numeral 3 is given in nos. [3] and [9] at the beginning of the passage and as a supplementary figure before each ternary group. In no. [20] the numeral 3 introduces ternary groups of white minims. Sesquialtera proportion is shown in the scores by the bracketed time signature $\frac{3}{2}$ and by a sign of equivalence above the top staff: **o**=**o·**. The first value in the equation refers to the normal (imperfect) semibreve and the second to the perfect semibreve in the proportion. Coloration is indicated by open brackets (⌐ ¬), while ligatures are marked by closed brackets above the notes involved (⌐——¬).

To bring forward the care composers took in observing natural text accents, I have used a method of accentual barring. Editorial barlines generally mark off material in regular groups of two beats per unit but may be extended to include three beats when text accents fall in irregular positions. Barlines function as markers of textual-temporal units and should not be construed as calling for pronounced downbeats. The tactus remains constant in the temporal units $\frac{2}{2}$, $\frac{3}{2}$, and occasionally $\frac{4}{2}$. When the $\frac{3}{2}$ symbol denotes a proportion, it is always set off by a sign of equivalence. A typical eleven-syllable line of *villanesca* poetry contains a pattern of accents in varying strengths. The principal (tonic) accent falls on the penultimate or tenth syllable, while secondary accents occur on the sixth, fourth, or second syllables. In shorter refrain lines of five, seven, or nine syllables, the principal accent also falls on the penultimate syllable. In general composers set stressed syllables to longer rhythmic values that often coincide with points of structural significance in the dominant melodic line. The insertion of barlines is determined by the hierarchy of text accents and the melodic structure of the tune-bearing voice. It is a flexible procedure, and often more than one solution is possible. Barlines have been distributed with particular attention to the principal accent, which composers normally underscored with dominant harmony and a syncopated dissonance. Resolution on the tonic coincides with an unaccented syllable occurring in a weak temporal position, thus giving rise to the so-called feminine cadence. But these cadences often cross the barline when the duration of the tonic chord is prolonged, producing a musical "misaccentuation" that diminishes the effect of the principal text accent.[122] Secondary text accents usually fall in the strong position of $\frac{3}{2}$ units, which more often than not precede suspension–resolution cadences. Sometimes, however, secondary accents are placed in the weaker portion of

a unit so that the principal accent can be allocated its proper position. Units in $\frac{3}{2}$ occasionally contain syncopated patterns to reflect alternating strong–weak accents imposed by the composer whether or not the diction is accurate.

Modern transcriptions of intabulations have been barred like their vocal models. Barring in the three-voice *villanesche* does not always correspond to Lasso's arrangements because of variance in text setting. Identical barring systems have been maintained in repeated phrases, even though minor deviations at the end of a second statement sometimes preclude the most effective barring. Repeated phrases have been written out as in the sources. Exceptions are nos. [18], [21], and [23]. The final chord of each composition always has the value of a longa in the sources. It is signified here by a fermata, and its value has been reinterpreted to complete whatever cadential pattern might be present in a balanced manner. In multistrophic compositions the final chord should be precisely measured for the sake of a smooth transition to the next strophe. Its ultimate value, however, can be sung as given or extended ad libitum.

Composers' signs for accidentals are placed directly before the notes to which they apply and, in accordance with modern convention, are valid for the entire measure unless cancelled by a subsequent accidental. Where the cancelling accidental has been added editorially as a consequence of modern convention, it is placed in the staff in square brackets. In pieces with a B-flat signature, the modern natural sign of cancellation has been substituted for the sharp in the source without comment. Source accidentals are assumed to apply to all immediate repetitions of the same pitch. When a modern barline intervenes in such a series, the accidental has been repeated in the staff and enclosed in square brackets. (For more information on conventions followed by sixteenth-century printers in marking accidentals, see Texts, Translations, and Commentary under "Music Reports.") All other editorial accidentals are placed above the pitches to which they apply and are valid only for the note so marked. If they serve a cautionary function, they are enclosed in parentheses. The application of *musica ficta* has been guided by sixteenth-century conventions as follows: to avoid augmented fourths, diminished fifths, and augmented and diminished octaves; and to raise the seventh degree at cadences.

All given strophes of a poem have been underlaid. Underlay of the first strophe presents few editorial problems since its prosody determined the composer's setting. Difficulties do arise, however, in underlaying the remaining strophes, which often do not fit the music as neatly as the first. Redistribution of stresses and addition or deletion of syllables call for solutions that cannot always be consistent with the underlay of the first strophe, especially when repeated notes on the same pitch are present. To compensate for added or deleted syllables, dashed ties are supplied. Since singers would have taken liberties in fitting text to music during Lasso's time, editorial underlay should be considered as a recommendation, not a definitive solution. Truncated words are set off by ellipsis. When partial or full repetition of a phrase is indicated by *ij* in the source, the text is editorially supplied in angle brackets.

Instrumental Compositions

Intabulations for fretted instruments have been transcribed from editions with the most accurate readings. Only a representative selection from the complete corpus of Lasso's intabulated *villanesche* is included here, because for some compositions the intabulators, using different tablatures and fingerings, produced nearly identical results. Each intabulation is presented in diplomatic transcription on a staff parallel to its modern transcription in staff notation. Ciphers in the Italian tablatures are placed directly on the lines as in the original sources. Letters in the French tablatures, originally on lines, are placed in the spaces between lines for greater legibility. Two systems for indicating duration are present in the original tablatures. In one the metrical signs are given separately (i.e., flagged signs are not beamed together), and a given sign obtains until a new one is called for. In the other, flagged signs are beamed together, and the same sign is usually repeated until a new one is needed. To establish a consistent format for the reproduction of metrical signs in the diplomatic transcriptions, the first system described above was adopted for all compositions. The plain vertical stroke denotes the semibreve, and strokes with one to four flags the minim, semiminim, croma, and semicroma, respectively. The transcriptions are based on standard sixteenth-century tunings, which are noted at the head of the scores. (French tunings are to be read from bottom course to top, while Italian tunings read from top course to bottom.) When an additional lute course is required, its tuning is shown below the tablature (e.g., in no. [31] "VII:C" means that the seventh course is tuned to C).

In reproducing the tablatures, obvious errors and omissions in the sources have been emended. Editorial emendations are bracketed in the tablature and transcription. The location and nature of an error is specified in the critical notes, where the strings of fretted instruments are designated by pitch name according to the familiar system wherein c′ = middle C, c = the C below middle C, and so on, and letters and ciphers are set off by italics. Some errors are obvious mistakes and stand corrected by internal analogy or by analogy with the vocal model. Others appear to be errors according to the model but are not corrected because they represent personal preferences of the intabulator or adaptations arising from limitations of the instrument.

Transcriptions inevitably transmit the editor's implicit view of a given texture as well as an opinion on the intended relationship between intabulation and model.[123] Mine bring forward the intabulator's consistent projection of Lasso's homophonic textures; hence, stems and beams define the texture as chordal with the highest note of a chord normally being the superius of the model. Intabulations for four-course cittern are transcribed on a single staff. The accompanying parts are joined on a single downward stem for the most part, and the superius is set off by an upward stem. Intabulations for lute and six-course cittern are represented by keyboard realizations in bi-stave transcriptions. Notes are held to allowable durations, especially when open strings are involved, and rests are added sparingly for clarification. Cautionary accidentals are given in parentheses on the staff. The open scores in the keyboard manuscript Coimbra 242 are here reduced to two staves and the original barring in semibreves retained. Bracketed accidentals on the staff replace what appear to be erroneous omissions. However, the scribe may have assumed some convention of prolonged validity, for example, that accidentals marked in a phrase would also be valid when the phrase was repeated.

Acknowledgments

As on a number of previous occasions, I am indebted to the Graduate School of the University of Minnesota and the Putnam Dana McMillan Committee for research and travel grants that made funds available for timely completion of this edition. I should especially like to acknowledge the contributions of my graduate research assistants, Steven Krantz and Joe Hagedorn, who copied much of the music (before the advent of music processors) and offered countless practical suggestions in matters of editing. I owe thanks to the staffs of many European libraries for their prompt attention to my requests for microfilms: Berleburg, Fürstlich Sayn-Wittgenstein-Berleburgsche Bibliothek; Berlin, Staatsbibliothek der Preußischer Kulturbesitz; Bologna, Civico Museo Bibliografico Musicale; Brussels, Bibliothèque Royale Albert Ier; Coimbra, Universidade de Coimbra, Biblioteca Geral; Kassel, Deutsches Musikgeschichtliches Archiv; London, The British Library; Munich, Bayerische Staatsbibliothek; Paris, Bibliothèque Nationale; Rostock, Universitäts-Bibliothek; Strasbourg, Union Sainte Cecile; Uppsala, Universitetsbiblioteket; Winchester, Winchester College

Warden and Fellows' Library; Wolfenbüttel, Herzog August Bibliothek; Wroclaw, Biblioteka Uniwersytecka; Vienna, Österreichische Nationalbibliothek; Zurich, Zentralbibliothek. Among American libraries I am indebted to the University of Minnesota (especially Katherine Holum of the Music Library and the interlibrary loan experts of the Wilson Library), the Newberry Library in Chicago, and the University of Illinois Musicological Archives for Renaissance Manuscript Studies.

Others helped in immeasurable ways: Vera Rabai checked the translations and Robert Laudon the keyboard scores; my husband, David Jackson, shared the pleasure and the pain of conquering the word processor. I am deeply appreciative of the patient and thorough editorial effort of Aaron Appelstein in seeing this book through the press. It is fitting that I dedicate this edition with gratitude and affection to the students who were members of the University of Minnesota Ensemble for Early Music during its preparation. For their patience in experimenting with mixed ensemble arrangements and their lively sense of musical humor (exceeded only by Lasso's), I am grateful.

Donna G. Cardamone

Notes

1. Adolf Sandberger edited the complete corpus of dialect songs in Orlando di Lasso, *Sämtliche Werke*, vol. 10, *Madrigale*, pt. 5 (Leipzig: Breitkopf & Härtel, 1898). The *morescas*, *todescas*, and *dialogues* in *Libro de villanelle* are omitted from the present edition.

2. Horst Leuchtmann, *Orlando di Lasso*, vol. 1, *Sein Leben* (Wiesbaden: Breitkopf & Härtel, 1976), and vol. 2, *Briefe* (Wiesbaden: Breitkopf & Härtel, 1977).

3. Ignace Bossuyt, ed., *Orlandus Lassus, 1532–1594* [exhibition catalogue] (Louvain: Uitgeverij Acco, 1982); Horst Leuchtmann and Helmut Hell, eds., *Orlando di Lasso: Musik der Renaissance am Münchner Fürstenhof, Ausstellung zum 450. Geburtstag, 27. Mai–31. Juli 1982*, Bayerische Staatsbibliothek, Ausstellungskataloge, 26 (Wiesbaden: Reichert, 1982); and *Revue belge de musicologie* 39–40 (1985–86), an issue devoted to papers presented at the Mons conference on Lasso in 1983.

4. Samuel van Quickelberg, "Orlandus de Lassus Musicus," in Heinricus Pantaleon, *Prosopographia Heroum atque Illustrium Virorum Totius Germaniae* (Basel, 1566), 3:541–42. For a facsimile reproduction, see Leuchtmann, *Orlando di Lasso* 1:298–300. Quickelberg, who was employed at the Munich court from 1553 to 1567, learned firsthand from Lasso about his life and career. However, Quickelberg could have been mistaken about Lasso's birthdate, since 1532 is equally plausible; Leuchtmann's review of the conflicting evidence allows no decision for one date or the other (*Orlando di Lasso* 1:72–81). This essay adopts the chronology Leuchtmann postulates for Lasso's life (ibid., 46–60); his biography supersedes all previous studies, whose erroneous and contradictory information he painstakingly corrects.

5. Nicolas Gombert, letter to Gonzaga, Tournai, 3 June 1547, reproduced in *Die Musik in Geschichte und Gegenwart*, s.v. "Gombert, Nicolas," by Joseph Schmidt-Görg. On Gonzaga's patronage of Titian, Leone Leoni, and Pietro Aretino, see Adolf Sandberger, *Orlando di Lasso und die geistigen Strömungen seiner Zeit* (Munich: R. Oldenbourg, 1926), 13.

6. Quickelberg, "Orlandus de Lassus Musicus," 541.

7. Gonzaga was in Mantua by 1 January according to a dispatch quoted by Federico Chabod, "L'epoca di Carlo V," in *Storia di Milano*, vol. 9 (Milan: Fondazione Trecciani degli Alfieri, 1961), 136. Gonzaga wrote to Pietro Aretino on 11 September from Mantua to explain that "the life-threatening illness of his wife had suspended all his other duties." Quoted in Sandberger, *Orlando di Lasso*, 11–12.

8. Adolf Sandberger, "Schicksale und Umgebung Orlando di Lasso's bis zu seinem Eintreffen am Münchener Hof, 1530 (1532)–1556," *Beiträge zur Geschichte der bayerischen Hofkapelle unter Orlando di Lasso*, vol. 1 (Leipzig: Breitkopf & Härtel, 1894), 85.

9. James Gairdner and R. H. Brodie, eds., *Letters and Papers, Foreign and Domestic of the Reign of Henry VIII*, vol. 19, pt. 2 (London: Her Majesty's Stationery Office, 1880), no. 568.

10. James Haar, "A Madrigal Falsely Ascribed to Lasso," *Journal of the American Musicological Society* 28 (1975): 529; and idem, "The Early Madrigals of Lassus," *Revue belge de musicologie* 39–40 (1985–86): 18–20.

11. On 3 July 1548 the retinues of Maximilian of Austria, son of the emperor's younger brother Ferdinand, and Cardinal Cristoforo Madruzzo of Trent converged at Milan on their way to Spain for Maximilian's marriage to the Infanta Maria, daughter of Charles V. Between 20 December 1548 and 7 January 1549, the emperor's son and heir, Philip II, made his triumphal entry into Milan. Then twenty-one years old, Philip was regent of Spain and on his first "goodwill" tour of Europe, eventually to be reunited with his father in Brussels.

12. Guglielmo Barblan, "La vita musicale in Milano nella prima metà del Cinquecento," in *Storia di Milano* 9:859–60; Bonner Mitchell, *The Majesty of the State: Triumphal Progresses of Foreign Sovereigns in Renaissance Italy* (Florence: Leo S. Olschki, 1986), 183–86.

13. Nino Pirrotta, *Music and Theatre from Poliziano to Monteverdi*, trans. Karen Eales (Cambridge: Cambridge University Press, 1982), 76–81.

14. On the question of Lasso's voice change in relation to the alleged birthdates, see Leuchtmann, *Orlando di Lasso* 1:75.

15. Lasso traveled to Naples with Constantino Castriota, a Neapolitan nobleman and writer who had served the imperial commander Alfonso d'Avalos as secretary (*Dizionario biografico degli italiani*, s.v. "Castriota, Constantino," by Renato Pastore). Between Gonzaga and Castriota, Lasso had ample opportunity to experience the values of the governing class and intellectual elite that would control his social life in Naples.

16. Gonzaga, it should be added, held many fiefs and titles in the kingdom of Naples acquired both by marriage to Isabella di Capua and in recognition of his loyalty to the crown. As commander of the Spanish cavalry during the French invasion of Naples in 1528, Gonzaga defended the city in life-threatening maneuvers, then in the following year reconquered lands in Puglia previously taken by the French. Traitorous barons who had joined the French army lost their fiefs to loyal commanders of Charles V, among them Gonzaga, who in 1532 acquired Alberigo Carafa's land in Principata Citra, his title duke of Ariano, and his residence in Naples. See Tommaso Pedio, *Napoli e Spagna nella prima metà del Cinquecento* (Bari: F. Cacucci, 1971), 225; and G. Capasso, "Don Ferrante Gonzaga all'impresa di Puglia del 1529," *Rivista storica italiana* 7 (1895): 419.

17. Bartolomeo Capasso, "Napoli descritta ne' principii del secolo XVII da Giulio Cesare Capaccio," *Archivio storico per le province napoletane* 7 (1883): 532.

18. Giuseppe Galasso, "Breve premessa alla storia civile e sociale di Napoli," in *Musica e cultura a Napoli del XV al XIX secolo*, ed. Lorenzo Bianconi and Renato Bossa (Florence: Leo S. Olschki, 1983), 23–25.

19. Benedetto Croce, *History of the Kingdom of Naples*, trans. Frances Frenaye (Chicago: University of Chicago Press, 1970), 116.

20. Quoted in Giuseppe Coniglio, "Note sulla società napoletana ai tempo di Don Pietro di Toledo," in *Studi in onore di Riccardo Filangieri*, vol. 2 (Naples: L'arte Tipografica, 1959), 347. See also Adelaide Mastrocinque, "Cinquecento napoletano," in *Storia di Napoli*, vol. 7 (Naples: Edizioni Scientifiche Italiane, 1980), 593–603.

21. Coniglio, "Note sulla società napoletana," 360, from a dispatch dated 23 January 1536.

22. On the Neapolitan *mascherata*, see Donna G. Cardamone, *The "Canzone villanesca alla napolitana" and Related Forms, 1537–1570*, 2 vols. (Ann Arbor: UMI Research Press, 1981), 1:148–52.

23. The term *musico* was used then to refer to musicians who did not belong to the nobility but whose social status was higher, for example, than that of instrumentalists hired to play for civic occasions. Keith Larsen, "Condizione sociale dei musicisti e dei loro committenti nella Napoli del Cinque e Seicento," in *Musica e cultura a Napoli*, ed. Bianconi and Bossa, 76.

24. Ibid., 72.

25. Coniglio, "Note sulla società napoletana," 359–60.

26. The most complete genealogy of d'Azzia's family is given in *Lettura di Girolamo Ruscelli sopra un sonetto dell'illustris. Signore Marchese della Terza* (Venice: G. Griffio, 1552), fols. 42r–44r. Cf. Eustachio d'Afflitto, *Memorie degli scrittori del regno di Napoli*, vol. 1 (Naples: Simoniana, 1782), 485–86; Carlo de Lellis, *Discorsi delle famiglie nobili del regno di Napoli*, vol. 3 (Naples: H. Saulo, 1671), 29, 174, 395.

27. In 1548 a castle in Laterza (Terra di Otranto) was restored by the d'Azzia family (*Puglia: Guida d'Italia del Touring Club Italiano* [Milan: Touring Club Italiano, 1962], 348). It is likely that Giovan Battista d'Azzia initiated this project because, according to Scipione Mazzella, the marquisate he inherited takes its name from this locality (*Descrittione del regno di Napoli* [Naples: G. B. Cappello, 1601], 7, 688). The title *della Terza* is derived from La Terza, an alternate spelling of Laterza. Both nomenclatures are used in Giovanni Antonio Magini, *Italia* (Bologna: S. Bonomi, 1620), tables 48 and 50.

28. Benedetto Croce, "I seggi di Napoli," in *Aneddoti di varia letteratura*, vol. 1 (Bari: G. Laterza, 1953), 298.

29. Haar, "The Early Madrigals of Lassus," 21–22.

30. Benedetto Croce, "Un sonetto dell'Aretino e un ritratto di Maria d'Aragona, marchesana del Vasto," in *Aneddoti di varia letteratura* 1:359–65. Ruscelli's *Lettura* (n. 26) is an academic reading of d'Azzia's sonnet with copious digressions on platonic love. His *Le imprese illustri* (Venice: F. de' Franceschi, 1580), 233–35, contains a commentary on d'Azzia's emblem, an eagle bitten in the heart by a dipsas serpent with the motto "semper ardentius." Ruscelli imputes the origin of the emblem to d'Azzia's insatiable thirst for a *paragone* whose identity is not disclosed.

31. Benedetto Croce, "L'accademia dei Sereni," in *Aneddoti di varia letteratura* 1:302–9. See also Camillo Minieri-Riccio, "Cenno storico delle accademie fiorite nella città di Napoli," *Archivio storico per le province napoletane* 5 (1880): 590–92.

32. The Neapolitan composer Tomaso Cimello specified in his *Libro primo de canti* (Venice: A. Gardane, 1548), 3, that a madrigal of his, *Veni giocosa a florida Thalia*, was sung as the introduction to a comedy played for the Sereni.

33. Benedetto Croce, "Farse, rappresentazioni sacre, egloghe e prime commedie regolari," in *I teatri di Napoli dal Rinascimento alla fine del secolo decimottavo* (Bari: G. Laterza, 1916), 21.

34. "Nell'anno 1545. Molti Gentiluomini Napoletani conchiusero di recitare una Commedia per loro esercizio, e per passatempo della Città. L'autor di questo fu il Signor Giovan Francesco Muscettola, uomo di belle lettere, ma di pronto, e mordace ingegno. E scelta la Commedia degl'Ingannati, opera degl'Intronati Accademici Senesi, con bellissimo apparato di lumi, di vesti, e di musica la rappresentorno nella Sala del Palazzo del Principe di Salerno, dove stava sempre per tal effetto apparecchiato il Proscenio. . . . Il Dentice, il Mariconda, e quel delle Palle rappresentorno i Servi con grazia mirabile: il Brancaccio, l'Innamorato assai bene: il Muscettola, Giglio Spagnuolo per maraviglia: Fabrizio Dentice figlio di Luigi, la Pasquella graziosamente: il Villano, un Pedante nobile, e grave: il Ricoveri, il Vecchio sciocco per impazzire: il Salernitano, il vecchio Virginio molto gravemente: un figlio della Signora Giovanna Palomba, il Fabio sopra modo aggarbato; e tutti gli altri dissero assai acconciamente; talchè Napoli non ebbe d'invidia punto a Siena per gli recitanti. Zoppino celebre Musico e giudizioso di quel tempo, ebbe cura della Musica scelta, ed anco dell'accordo degl'instrumenti; onde la Musica fu veramente celeste; e massime perchè il Dentice con il suo Falsetto, ed il Brancaccio col Basso ferno miracoli. L'anno seguente 1546. Si recitò un'altra Commedia, Opera del Mariconda, detta la Filenia, rappresentata da quasi tutti i medesimi recitanti con una eccellente Musica, che riuscì buonissima." Antonino Castaldo, *Dell'istoria di notar Antonino Castaldo libri quattro, ne' quali si descrivono gli avvenimenti più memorabili succeduti nel regno di Napoli sotto il governo del vicere D. Pietro di Toledo e de' vicerè suoi successori fino al Cardinal Granuelo* (Naples: G. Gravier, 1769), 71–72.

35. Pirrotta, *Music and Theatre*, 107–8.

36. Donna G. Cardamone, "The Debut of the *Canzone villanesca alla napolitana*," *Studi musicali* 4 (1975): 65–75.

37. Nola's first book of madrigals (1545) was dedicated to the merchant-banker Gioan Geronimo Ravaschiero. Doc-

umentation for Nola's life is scarce until he became *maestro di cappella* at the SS. Annunziata in 1563. See Cardamone, *The "Canzone villanesca"* 1:110–12.

38. The Florentine envoy Bernardo dei Medici reported that every night Sanseverino was surrounded by admiring ladies who "made him sing *napolitane* and accompanied him on a number of guitars, each lady having her own" ("li fanno cantare delle canzoni napolitane et ci hanno indocte una quantità di chitarre, ed ogni dama ha la sua"). Quoted in Benedetto Croce, "Isabella Villamarino," in *Aneddoti di varia letteratura* 1:334; and Ulisse Prota-Giurleo, "Musici napoletani del '500: Ferrante Sanseverino e il lamento di 'Donna Sabella,' " *Partenope* 2 (1961): 299.

39. For a short-title catalogue of *villanesca* prints from 1537 to 1570, see Cardamone, *The "Canzone villanesca"* 2:1–23.

40. James Haar, *Essays on Italian Poetry and Music in the Renaissance, 1350–1600* (Berkeley and Los Angeles: University of California Press, 1986), 90.

41. Dentice dedicated the first edition of his treatise to Brancaccio. References here are to the second edition (Rome: V. Lucrino, 1553), "Dialogo secondo," fol. 29r–v. Dentice was remembered posthumously as "first among Neapolitan lute nists" by Nicolo Tagliaferro, *L'esercitio*, fol. 83r (Naples, Biblioteca dei Gerolamini, MS. S.M. XXVIII.1.66).

42. Tomaso Cimello appears to have been in residence at the d'Aragona household ca. 1545. Domenico Gamucci reported that while visiting him there, he found him "in a bad mood because someone had stolen a bundle of his unpublished works." See Gamucci's dedication to Paolo del Rosso, *Regole, osservanze, et avvertenze sopra lo scrivere correttamente la lingua volgare Toscana in prosa e in versi* (Naples: M. Cancer, 1545). In a letter written near the end of his life (ca. 1579), Cimello recalled that "Orlando had come to see him," perhaps seeking a mentor. On Cimello's reputation as theorist and teacher, see Cardamone, *The "Canzone villanesca"* 1:106–9. Giovanni Camillo Maffei cited Cimello and Nola as the authorities on the courtly art of singing in the ornamented style in *Delle lettere* (Naples: R. Amato, 1562).

43. Giambattista Del Tufo, "Ritratto ò modello delle grandezze, delizie, e maraviglie della nobilissima città di Napoli" (1588), fol. 54r (Naples, Biblioteca Nazionale, MS. XII.C.96).

44. "Della musica poi, oltre di quel naturale instinto, di che par che il Cielo habbia ogni Napoletano spirito dotato, onde quasi ciascuno alla natura, l'arte giungendo di giorno, e di notte, tal'hora con voci, tal'hora con strumenti, diverse armonie in diversi luochi si sentono con dolcezza mirabile." Benedetto di Falco, *Antichità di Napoli e del suo amenissimo distretto*, 6th ed. (Naples: C. Porsile, 1679), 64. The first edition, printed in Naples by Mattia Cancer in 1535 under the title *Descrizione dei luoghi antichi di Napoli*, is lost.

45. "Che non si ha d'haver per inconveniente se in simil sorte di cantilene, imitatrice de quei aeri che trovano piu voce senza cognitione di Musica, . . . vediamo fare ad ogni sorte di persone che volendo cantare quel medemo verso, che canta un'altro; và cercando i suoni, & le voci delettevole, per rendere il canto simile al canto Musicale: onde possiamo credere che i Musici, vedendo queste operationi fatte mediante l'udito, & la natura: gl'habiano redutti a questa forma: che ben si vede quando le Villanelle, & l'altre cosette non sono semplici aeri: che tengano del Musicale, & sono fatte secondo le Musicali regole: ma che essendo di quella sorte d'aeri che io dico, vanno quei rozzi aeri imitando." Lodovico Zacconi, *Prattica di musica utile e necessaria* (Venice, 1596), bk. 1, fol. 81v.

46. Fernand Braudel, *The Mediterranean and the Mediterranean World in the Age of Philip II*, 2 vols. (New York: Harper and Row, 1972), 1:346. On demographic distribution of social classes and trades in Naples, see Claudia Petraccone, *Napoli dal Cinquecento all'Ottocento: Problemi di storia demografica e sociale* (Naples: Guida, 1974), 90–93.

47. Giuseppe Coniglio, *Il regno di Napoli al tempo di Carlo V* (Naples: Edizioni Scientifiche Italiane, 1951), 149.

48. Haar, *Essays*, 118. Einstein's notion that *villanesca* composers intentionally parodied the refined polyphony and platonic idealization of the madrigal (*The Italian Madrigal*, 3 vols. [Princeton, N.J.: Princeton University Press, 1949], 1:374) has been opposed by Pirrotta (*Music and Theatre*, 111). The relationship between the genres is more satisfactorily explained as complementary than as antagonistic.

49. Leuchtmann, *Orlando di Lasso* 1:87–92. St. John Lateran was then the location of the papacy's most important public ceremonial occasions.

50. This episode in Lasso's life has raised a number of interpretations, summarized in ibid., 92–96.

51. For further information, see Kristine K. Forney, "Orlando di Lasso's 'Opus 1': The Making and Marketing of a Renaissance Music Book," *Revue belge de musicologie* 39–40 (1985–86): 35–37; and Franzpeter Messmer, *Ein Leben in der Renaissance: Orlando di Lasso* (Munich: Edition Wissenschaft und Literatur, 1982), 73–76.

52. See Corpus of Early Music, 15 (Brussels: Editions Culture et Civilisation, 1972), for a facsimile of the exemplar held at Munich, Bayerische Staatsbibliothek.

53. Forney, "Orlando di Lasso," 41–43; Donna G. Cardamone and David L. Jackson, "Multiple Formes and Vertical Setting in Susato's First Edition of Lassus's 'Opus 1,' " *Notes* 46 (1989): 7–24.

54. This possibility was first raised by Leuchtmann and Hell, eds., *Orlando di Lasso*, 123, and confirmed by Forney, "Orlando di Lasso," 43–47. For the full titles of the books that constitute the first edition, see the Key to Sigla and Abbreviations.

55. Forney, "Orlando di Lasso," 45–47.

56. Guido Persoons, "Orlandus Lassus in Antwerpen (1554–1556)," in *Orlandus Lassus*, ed. Bossuyt, 73. For a translation of the dedication, see Forney, "Orlando di Lasso," 37.

57. Forney, "Orlando di Lasso," 38.

58. Ibid., 47–48.

59. See *The New Grove Dictionary of Music and Musicians*, s.v. "Le Roy, Adrian," by Samuel F. Pogue.

60. For a full account of Lasso's privileges and relationships with his publishers, see Henri Vanhulst, "Lassus et ses éditeurs: Remarques à propos de deux lettres peu connues," *Revue belge de musicologie* 39–40 (1985–86): 80–100.

61. Henri Vanhulst, "De Leuvense Lassusdrukken van het Uitgeversbedrijf Phalesius (1560–1578)," in *Orlandus Lassus*, ed. Bossuyt, 87.

62. Ibid., 88.

63. *Census-Catalogue of Manuscript Sources of Polyphonic Music, 1400–1550*, Compiled by the University of Illinois Musicological Archives for Renaissance Manuscript Studies, vol. 4, ed. Charles Hamm and Herbert Kellman, Renaissance Manuscript Studies, 1 (Neuhausen-Stuttgart: Hanssler-Verlag, 1988), 135–36. The provenance of the manuscript was established by Jerry Call.

64. *The New Grove Dictionary of Music and Musicians*, s.v. "Kargel, Sixt," by Wolfgang Boetticher and Hans Radke.

65. *The New Grove Dictionary of Musical Instruments*, s.v. "Cittern," by James Tyler.

66. Santiago Kastner, "Los manuscritos musicales nº 48 y 242 de la Biblioteca General de la Universidad de Coimbra," *Anuario musical* 5 (1950): 78–96.

67. Forney, "Orlando di Lasso," 51–54. All the other pieces by Lasso in Coimbra 242 were drawn from "Opus I."

68. This volume, previously believed lost, has recently been located at the Biblioteka Jagiellońska in Kracow: *Canzoni villanesche de Don Ioan Domenico del Giovane de Nola, libro primo et secondo, novamente stampati* (Venice: G. Scotto, 1541). See Mary S. Lewis, *Antonio Gardano, Venetian Music Printer, 1538–1569: A Descriptive Bibliography and Historical Study*, vol. 1 (New York: Garland, 1988), 475–76.

69. Nino Pirrotta, "Willaert and the *Canzone villanesca*," in *Music and Culture in Italy from the Middle Ages to the Baroque: A Collection of Essays* (Cambridge: Harvard University Press, 1984), 195.

70. "Coloro che non sanno di Musica . . . non hanno riguardo (perche non sanno) di fare non solo due ò piu quinte. . . . Che trovandosi in simil consonanze, ne i moti propinqui non si sanno altrimente movere: perche si sentono essere accompagnati bene." Zacconi, *Prattica di musica*, bk. 1, fol. 81v.

71. Nino Pirrotta, "New Glimpses of an Unwritten Tradition," in *Music and Culture*, 58.

72. Donna G. Cardamone, "Forme musicali e metriche della canzone villanesca e della villanella alla napolitana," *Rivista italiana di musicologia* 12 (1977): 59–66.

73. Pirrotta, "Willaert," 181–82.

74. See Adrian Willaert et al., *Canzone Villanesche alla Napolitana and Villotte*, ed. Donna G. Cardamone, Recent Researches in the Music of the Renaissance, vol. 30 (Madison: A-R Editions, 1978), xv–xvii.

75. "Sarebbe stato piu conveniente che io havessi pubblicato queste mie Villanelle in mia gioventù, nel qual tempo io le feci, che publicarle in questa età grave, nella quale io mi truovo: per il che io non havevo punto l'animo disposto a mandarle in luce, mà gli amici me n'hanno tanto astretto, ch'io sono stato sforzato di seguir piu tosto la volontà loro che il giudicio mio."

76. The earliest known source for the model of '*Sto core mio* is RISM 156012. For *O occhi manza mia*, it is RISM 155720, published in Rome. These compositions must have been in circulation before their publication ('*Sto core mio* certainly before 1555) and could have been composed by Lasso himself.

77. Wolfgang Boetticher, *Orlando di Lasso und seine Zeit, 1532–1594* (Kassel: Bärenreiter, 1958), 495–97, 511–15.

78. James Haar, "False Relations and Chromaticism in Sixteenth-Century Music," *Journal of the American Musicological Society* 30 (1977): 406.

79. Croce, *History of the Kingdom of Naples*, 116.

80. Arturo Graf, "Una cortigiana fra mille: Veronica Franco," *Attraverso il Cinquecento* (Turin: E. Loescher, 1916), 251.

81. Georgina Masson, *Courtesans of the Italian Renaissance* (London: Secker and Warburg, 1975), 140.

82. Norman M. Penzer, ed. and trans., *The Pentamerone of Giambattista Basile*, 2 vols. (London: John Lane, 1932), 1:121.

83. "E quella che non ne havesse saputo una frotta de le più belle e de le più nuove se ne saria vergognata." Pietro Aretino, *Capricciosi & piacevoli raggionamenti* (Amsterdam: Elzevier, 1660), pt. 2, 391.

84. Masson, *Courtesans*, 139.

85. Thomas Caldecot Chubb, *Aretino: Scourge of Princes* (New York: Reynal and Hitchcock, 1940), 360.

86. Ibid., 353.

87. Quoted in ibid., 359.

88. Wolfgang Boetticher, *Aus Orlando di Lassos Wirkungskreis* (Kassel: Bärenreiter, 1963), 22, 24–25.

89. "Messer Orlando di Lasso, con li suoi cantori, a tutti lassa il freno, che con suave e piana voce, facciano udir le compositioni, che ciascun giorno di nuovo li presenta. Et al spesso, (non senza gran sodisfattione del Duca) fa cantare alcuni belli quarti, & artificiosi terzi, da prattici e scelti Cantori: che posso giurare haver visto sua Eccellenza lassare il Prandio per udir la harmonia." Horst Leuchtmann, *Die Münchner Fürstenhochzeit von 1568: Massimo Troiano, Dialoge* (Munich: E. Katzbichler, 1980), 104–6. On Troiano, see pp. 437–39.

90. Boetticher, *Orlando di Lasso*, 583–84; and Wolfgang Boetticher, "Über einige in jüngerer Zeit hinzugewonnene Sätze Orlando di Lassos," *Revue belge de musicologie* 39–40 (1985–86): 76.

91. "Venne in fantasia all'Illustriss. Duca Guglielmo di Baviera, di sentir una comedia il di seguente, & fece chiamare Orlando Lasso, ch'ad ogni cosa lo conoscea atto . . . trovò per sorte Massimo Troiano, nel la avanti camera . . . e cosi trovato il suggetto, e tra ambidue composero le parole." Leuchtmann, *Fürstenhochzeit*, 310.

92. Kathleen Marguerite Lea, *Italian Popular Comedy: A Study in the Commedia dell'arte, 1560–1620, with Special Reference to the English Stage*, 2 vols. (Oxford: Clarendon Press, 1934), 1:9.

93. "Da l'altra parte de la scena usci Orlando Lasso vestito da Magnifico con uno giubbone di raso cremesino, con calze di scarlato fatte alla Venetiana, & una vesta nera lunga infino a' piedi, e con una maschera che in vederla forzava le genti a ridere; con un liuto alle mani sonando e cantando, Chi passa per questa strada e non sospira beato sè; e dopò che l'hebbe replicato due volte; lassò il lauto e cominciò a lamentarsi dell' amore, & a dire, o povero Pantalon, che per questa strada non puol passare senza mandar sospiri all'aria, e lagrime al suolo de la terra." Leuchtmann, *Fürstenhochzeit*, 312.

94. Adolf Sandberger, "Orlando di Lassos Beziehungen zur italienischen Literatur," *Ausgewählte Aufsätze zur Musikgeschichte*, vol. 1 (Munich: Drei Masken Verlag, 1921), 60–61.

95. Leuchtmann, *Fürstenhochzeit*, 306.

96. Peter Röckl, "Das Musikleben am Hofe Wilhelms V. auf der Burg Trausnitz von 1568–1579," *Verhandlungen des historischen Vereins für Niederbayern* 99 (1973): 115–16.

97. Two standard works on this subject, but centered on Italian practices, are Emilie Elsner, *Untersuchung der instrumentalen Besetzungspraxis der weltlichen Musik im 16. Jahrhundert in Italien* (Ohlau: H. Eschenhagen, 1935); and Howard Mayer Brown, *Sixteenth-Century Instrumentation: The Music for the Florentine Intermedii*, Musicological Studies and Documents, 30 ([Rome:] American Institute of Musicology, 1973).

98. Howard Mayer Brown, *Embellishing Sixteenth-Century Music* (London: Oxford University Press, 1976), xi.

99. See Howard Mayer Brown, "Accidentals and Ornamentation in Sixteenth-Century Intabulations of Josquin's Motets," *Josquin des Prez*, ed. Edward E. Lowinsky and Bonnie J. Blackburn (London: Oxford University Press, 1976), 476.

100. Brown, *Sixteenth-Century Instrumentation*, 74.

101. Quoted from Troiano's *Dialoghi* by Clive Wearing, "Orlandus Lassus (1532–1594) and the Munich Kapelle," *Early Music* 10 (1982): 149.

102. Jürgen Eppelsheim, "Musikinstrumente zur Zeit Orlando di Lassos," in *Orlando di Lasso*, ed. Leuchtmann and Hell, 76–87.

103. For a facsimile of the title page, see Howard Mayer Brown, *Instrumental Music Printed before 1600: A Bibliography* (Cambridge: Harvard University Press, 1967), 279.

104. Quoted from *Il primo libro di tabolatura di citthara* (1574), in *The New Grove Dictionary of Musical Instruments*, s.v. "Cittern," by James Tyler.

105. Eppelsheim, "Musikinstrumente," 79.

106. Brown, *Sixteenth-Century Instrumentation*, 78–81.

107. Eppelsheim, "Musikinstrumente," 78–79.

108. Besides the works by Brown already cited, see also Timothy J. McGee, *Medieval and Renaissance Music: A Performer's Guide* (Toronto: University of Toronto Press, 1985).

109. Elsner, *Untersuchung*, 61–63, 88–89, documents Italian court festivities that featured pure, mixed, and soloistic ensembles, even in multiple renditions of the same composition.

110. Brown, *Embellishing*, 56–57.

111. See, for example, no. [19], m. 15, where an identical melodic interval is marked.

112. For an edition of Adriansen's arrangement for three lutes, transposed down a whole tone, see Godelieve Spiessens, ed., *Luitmuziek van Emanuel Adriaenssen*, Monumenta Musicae Belgicae, vol. 10 (Antwerp: Vereniging voor Muziekgeschiedenis, 1966), 85.

113. Godelieve Spiessens, "Emmanuel Adriaenssen et son Pratum Musicum," *Acta Musicologica* 36 (1964): 142–51; and Joan Myers, "Performance Practice Indications in Emanuel Adriansen's Lute Ensemble Music," *Journal of the Lute Society of America* 2 (1969): 18–27.

114. The normal Italian harpsichord of the sixteenth century was a single-manual instrument with two sets of eight-foot strings.

115. Andrew Parrott, "Transposition in Monteverdi's Vespers of 1610: An 'Aberration' Defended," *Early Music* 12 (1984): 496, cites keyboard and lute intabulations before 1600 (especially Adriansen's *Pratum Musicum*) that show transposition of high-clef pieces down a fourth or fifth.

116. Cardamone, The *"Canzone villanesca"* 1:162–69.

117. Howard Mayer Brown, "A Cook's Tour of Ferrara in 1529," *Rivista italiana di musicologia* 10 (1975): 237–41.

118. Röckl, "Das Musikleben," 91–97, 101–16.

119. James Haar, "The *Note Nere* Madrigal," *Journal of the American Musicological Society* 18 (1965): 24–25; Don Harrán, ed., *The Anthologies of Black-Note Madrigals*, Corpus Mensurabilis Musicae, 73 (Neuhausen-Stuttgart: American Institute of Musicology, Hanssler-Verlag, 1978), xiv.

120. Henry William Kaufmann, *The Life and Works of Nicola Vicentino (1511–c. 1576)*, Musicological Studies and Documents, 11 ([Rome:] American Institute of Musicology, 1966), 151.

121. Tomaso Cimello, *Regole nove* (ca. 1545), fols. 94v–95r (Naples, Biblioteca Nazionale MS VH 210). See also Harrán, ed., *Anthologies*, xiv.

122. Lasso's *La cortesia* (no. [1]) and *'No giorno* (no. [3]) are barred regularly in semibreves to match the system used in their keyboard intabulations. Feminine cadences fall within the bar in *La cortesia* but cross the barline in *'No giorno*.

123. Thomas F. Heck, "Lute Music: Tablatures, Textures and Transcriptions," *Journal of the Lute Society of America* 7 (1974): 24–27.

Texts, Translations, and Commentary

Introduction

TRANSCRIPTIONS OF TEXTS

The poems are given in the order in which their settings appear in the edition and in a format that clarifies their metrical form. Strophes are numbered to correspond to the numbering system in the scores. A principle of highest priority in transcribing the poems is the retention of their original orthography. Modernizing and regularizing spelling obliterates a hallmark of *villanesca* style, namely, the deliberate mixture of Italian and Neapolitan expressions and the vacillation between them that occurs during transmission. Neapolitan and Italian forms of a given word are often found in different sources of the same poem (e.g., *mietti/metti* and *contiento/contento*). Dialect words, too, are susceptible to variant spellings (e.g., *ce 'ncappi/ce 'ncapi* and *cha/ca*). Throughout the repertory the verb form *haggio* (first person, present indicative of *avere*) vacillates with *aggio*. Even though these two forms are phonetically identical (the *h* is silent), they have not been resolved into a common spelling. Spelling variants can also provide information about the preferences of printers and their editors or typesetters, who considered some spellings to be acceptable and others not, often bringing a composer's text in line with what they thought was correct or compatible with the regional market in question. But it is difficult to know whether a text variant originated with Lasso "improving" on a model or with a printer cleaning up a copy text. Only the most obvious typographical errors have been emended (with report in "Notes on the Text"). What often appear to be grammatical mistakes are actually loose constructions characteristic of popular poetry, for example, feminine instead of masculine endings and inversions of *voi* and *tu* forms. These deviations as well as irregularities in the rhyme scheme do not represent corruptions in the usual sense.

Punctuation is minimal or sometimes entirely absent in the sources under consideration and, when present, is rarely in agreement with modern usage. To clarify the meaning of the texts, punctuation marks have been editorially supplied in the text transcriptions and music underlay according to modern conventions. Addition of apostrophes and accents in the transcription of Neapolitan texts differs widely among editors. In my transcriptions and music underlay, I have followed the criteria formulated by Mario Petrini in his edition of Basile's early seventeenth-century Neapolitan works (Bas.C, 607–9) because there is linguistic continuity between the *villanesca* and later dialect literature. (For bibliographic abbreviations used in Texts, Translations, and Commentary, see the Key to Sigla and Abbreviations below.) Apostrophes, applied sparingly in the sources, normally signify elision—dropping the final vowel in a word when it precedes a word-initial vowel. When these apostrophes follow modern usage, they are retained in the transcription, but when superfluous they are suppressed. When one polyphonic part contains elided words and another does not, both are left unchanged in the text underlay of the score; the text transcription generally gives the elided reading. Apocopation, dropping a final vowel or syllable before another word—whether it begins with a vowel or a consonant—is common in Neapolitan dialect, particularly in verb forms. Truncated verb forms are rarely signified by an apostrophe in music sources. Hence, indispensable apostrophes are editorially supplied and generally not reported, for example, to distinguish *si'* (*sii, sia*) from *si*. Aferesis, the loss of one or more sounds at the beginning of a word, is characteristic of southern Italian dialects. Apostrophes signifying aferesis are rare or variable in music sources. They have been editorially supplied (without report) when needed to distinguish words spelled the same but with different meanings, for example, *'sto* (aferesis of the demonstrative adjective *questo*) and *sto* (first person singular, present indicative of *stare*). Accents are normally lacking in the sources on words where they are essential to clarify meaning or pronunciation, for example, *e/è* and *pieta/pietà*. They are added to conform to modern practice. Accents present in a poem are retained and a note supplied to that effect; occasional superfluous accents are deleted without report.

TRANSLATIONS, ANNOTATIONS, AND TEXT REPORTS

I have provided literal translations of the poems, retaining the original word order and syntax as closely as transference from one language to another permits. To convey colloquial speech patterns, I have made consistent use of contracted verbs and tried to find pithy equivalents for slang expressions and ono-matopoetic syllables. Neapolitan poets relied on pro-verbial, euphemistic, and metaphorical expressions from everyday language that present difficulties in translation when they carry double meanings or are purposefully ambiguous. Puns and witty forms of wordplay are likewise problematic and defy equiva-lents when the sound of the word in the original lan-guage is the carrier of meaning. Thus, the poems are annotated to clarify obscure meanings and regional allusions. (Annotations are signaled by footnote ref-erences in the poem and are given in "Notes on the Text.") My intention is to reveal at least the surface meaning of a poem in the translation and then to treat subtle implications in "Notes on the Text." The notes also document the *villanesca* poet's stock-in-trade of proverbial lore and the idiomatic spoken language. Many popular sayings in *villanesche* can be traced to proverb collections and Neapolitan works of a slightly later date whose authors were also consciously de-pendent on colloquial speech. Neapolitan words are defined by their Italian equivalents in the notes. The infinitive form is cited for verbs; variant or corrupt spellings of dialect words are identified as alternative spellings (abbreviated "alt. sp.") and are regularized in the notes to conform to modern usage. Highlight-ing the Neapolitan elements in this systematic man-ner permits the reader to retrace the translator's steps; it also indicates the proportionate level of Ne-apolitan words in any given poem. This data is useful in locating vacillation between standard and dialect forms of the same word in different readings. The "Notes on the Text" also report variants and errors affecting performance, for example, the number of strophes present in a given source and the status of refrain cues. Errors in "Opus I" compositions are re-ported only from Susato's editions, because they doc-ument the quality of editorial supervision. Numerous misspelled words in sources printed or copied after 1560 are not reported because they are "accidental" rather than significant errors.

MUSIC REPORTS

Obvious errors in the main source are corrected in the score, and the location and nature of the error are specified in "Notes on the Music." Variants and er-rors in concordant sources are also given. Pitch des-ignation follows the familiar system wherein c' = middle C, c = C below middle C, and so on. Names of partbooks correspond to those used in the sources (e.g., Superius in RISM 1555[19] but Canto in Lasso 1581). Accidentals in the sources present special prob-lems that warrant further explanation. Over the en-tire range of sources consulted, printers followed the convention of marking every note requiring an acci-dental except in a series of repeated notes on the

same pitch. Given the latter situation, they normally marked only the first note in the series; this accidental then continued to have validity for each successive note of the same pitch. When a modern barline in-tervenes in such a series, the accidental has been re-peated in the staff and enclosed in square brackets. In some cases a printer marked the second as well as the first note in a series, presumably to avoid ambi-guity. If the second accidental is redundant by mod-ern convention, its presence in the source is reported to document the intervention of a careful printer. The note supplied to this effect reads "accidental before." When a rest interrupts a series of repeated pitches with the first duly signed, the note following the rest does not always have an accidental in the source. Being a potentially ambiguous situation, the presence or absence of an accidental in this position is cited in the critical notes (the former by the phrase "acciden-tal before," the latter by the phrase "no accidental"). This same system of reports is used in other contexts where the prolonged validity of an accidental within the editorial measure obscures the presence or ab-sence of a repeated accidental assumed by the editor and required by normal source procedures. Where prolonged validity obviates the application of *musica ficta*, however, no report is given for the note so af-fected. Reports containing the phrase "accidental lacking" (as opposed to the phrase "no accidental") refer to the omission of an accidental as a variant or an error in setting type or copying.

In the lute and cittern intabulations (though not the keyboard intabulations), editorial emendations to the source are signaled by square brackets in both the diplomatic transcription and the accompanying mod-ern transcription in staff notation. The location and nature of the error, however, are specified only for the tablature reading and are reported in the critical notes. Pitch designations for the open strings of fret-ted instruments follows the familiar system in which middle C is c'. Emendations are located with refer-ence to (1) the measure number(s) of the modern transcription; (2) the vertical placement of notes within chords—numbered from bottom to top for pieces in French tablature and from top to bottom for pieces in Italian tablature; and (3) the horizontal placement of notes within "beats"—whereby the "beat" is defined in terms of the half note (minim) and chords are counted as single notes within a beat.

SOURCES

The main source and internal location for each composition are identified immediately after the text transcription. When only one exemplar of a source is extant and there are no concordant sources, a com-position is marked unicum. Locations of composi-tions within concordant sources are cited under the heading "Concordance(s)." The concordances themselves are listed in chronological order. The main source of Lasso's *villanesche* is Susato's *Le quatoirsiesme livre* (RISM 1555[19]), and for his *villanelle* it is Le Roy and Ballard's edition *Libro de villanelle* (1581). The Neapolitan models are drawn variously from the following sources: Fontana 1545, Nola 1545(1), Nola 1545(2), and RISM 1565[11]. (Gardano's reprints of 1545 were used as the main sources of Nola's *villanesche* because Scotto's earlier edition of 1541 could not be consulted; see note 68 above.) Not all concordances known to exist in printed sources were collated, because comparison across the entire spectrum of sources showed that in any given ancestral series reissues from the same press were reprints that rarely contained substantive alterations. These reissues serve primarily to corroborate errors and variants that were transmitted unnoticed from one early edition to the next. Collation beyond a third edition normally turned up insignificant variants. Hence, only substantive errors and variants from editions closest in line of descent to the first are reported. The first edition of *La fleur des chansons* (1592) could not be located; it is not at the Herzog August Bibliothek in Wolfenbüttel as reported in RISM A (L1002). Thus, the second edition of 1596 was collated. Because the second and final edition of *Continuation du mellange* (1596) contained no substantive revisions, it was not collated. Reports for the instrumental compositions contain collations of the main source with all extant concordant sources.

Key to Sigla and Abbreviations

Collections devoted to the works of a single composer are identified by sigla consisting of the composer's name and the date of publication. Anthologies containing works by more than one composer are identified by their number in RISM, series B/1. Only sources consulted are listed below. Extant partbooks are noted for each source (S = Superius or Canto; A = Contratenor or Alto; T = Tenor; B = Bassus).

PRINTED SOURCES OF VOCAL COMPOSITIONS

Cimello 1545 *Canzone villanesche al modo napolitano a tre voci di Thomaso Cimello da Napoli . . . libro primo.* Venice: A. Gardane, 1545 (S-T-B).

Fontana 1545 *Canzone villanesche di Vicenzo Fontana a tre voci alla napolitana novamente poste in luce, libro primo.* Venice: A. Gardane, 1545 (S-T-B).

Nola 1545(1) *Canzone villanesche de Don Ioan Domenico del Giovane de Nola, a tre voci novamente ristampate, libro primo.* Venice: A. Gardane, 1545 (S-T-B).

Nola 1545(2) *Canzone villanesche de Don Ioan Domenico del Giovane de Nola, a tre voci novamente ristampate, libro secundo.* Venice: A. Gardane, 1545 (S-T-B).

RISM 1555[19] *Le quatoirsiesme livre a quatre parties contenant, dixhuyct chansons italiennes, six chansons francoises, & six motetz, faictz (a la nouvelle composition d'aucuns d'Italie) par Rolando di Lassus.* Antwerp: T. Susato, 1555 (S-A-T-B).

RISM 1555[29] *D'Orlando di Lassus il primo libro dovesi contengono madrigali, vilanesche, canzoni francesi, e motetti a quattro voci.* Antwerp: T. Susato, 1555 (S).

RISM 1555[30] *Villanelle d'Orlando di Lassus e d'altri eccellenti musici libro secondo.* Rome: V. Dorico, 1555 (S); repr. RISM 1558[16] (T).

RISM 1557[20] *Secondo libro delle muse a tre voci. Canzon villanesche alla napolitana, di nuovo raccolte et date in luce.* Rome: A. Barré, 1557 (S).

[1558QL] *Le quatoirsiesme livre a quatre parties contenant dixhuyct chansons italiennes, six chansons francoises, & six motetz faictz (a la nouvelle composition d'aucuns d'Italie) par Rolando di Lassus.* Antwerp: T. Susato, 1555 [printed ca. 1558] (S-A-T-B).

RISM 1560[4] *Le quatoirsiesme livre a quatre parties contenant dixhuyct chansons italiennes, sept chansons francoises, & six motetz faictz (a la nouvelle composition d'aucuns d'Italie) par Rolando di Lassus.* Antwerp: T. Susato, 1560 (S-A-T-B).

RISM 1560[12] *Il primo libro delle villotte alla napolitana de diversi eccellentissimi authori novamente stampato. A tre voci.* Venice: A. Gardane, 1560 (S-T); repr. RISM 1562[11] (T-B), RISM 1571[5] (S-T-B). See also RISM 1565[11].

RISM 1560[13] *Il secondo libro delle villotte alla napolitana de diversi con due moresche nuovamente stampate. A tre voci.* Venice: A. Gardane, 1560 (T); repr. RISM 1562[12] (T), RISM 1566[6] (S-T-B), RISM 1571[6] (S-T-B). See also RISM 1565[11].

RISM 1565[11] *Li quattro libri delle villotte alla napolitana a tre voci. De diversi eccellentissimi auttori con due moresche nuovamente ristampate e con diligenza corrette.* Venice: G. Scotto, 1565 (S-T-B).

Lasso 1565 *Dixhuictieme livre de chansons à quatre & à cinq parties par Orlande de Lassus.* Paris: A. Le Roy and R. Ballard, 1565 (A-T-B); repr. 1567 (T-B), 1570 (S-A-T-B), 1573 (S-A-B), 1576 (S-A-T-B), 1581 (S-T-B).

Lasso 1567 See Lasso 1565.

Lasso 1570 See Lasso 1565.

RISM 1570[6] *Second livre des chansons a quatre et cinq parties composées par Orlando di Lassus, Cyprien de Rore, et Philippe de Mons, de nouveau corrigées et emendées, convenables tant aux instrumens comme à la voix.* Louvain and Antwerp: P. Phalèse and J. Bellère, 1570 (S-A-T-B-5).

RISM 1571[5] See RISM 1560[12].

RISM 1571[6] See RISM 1560[13].

Lasso 1581 *Libro de villanelle, moresche, et altre canzoni, a 4. 5. 6. et 8. voci di Orlando di Lasso.* Paris: A. Le Roy and R. Ballard, 1581 (S-A-T-B).

Lasso 1582 *Libro de villanelle, moresche, et altre canzoni, a 4. 5. 6. et 8. voci di Orlando di Lasso.* Antwerp: P. Phalèse and J. Bellère, 1582 (S-A-T-B).

Lasso 1584 *Continuation du mellange d'Orlande de Lassus à 3. 4. 5. 6. et dix parties.* Paris: A. Le Roy and R. Ballard, 1584 (S-A-T-B-5); repr. 1596 (S-A-T-B-5), 1597 (S-A-T-B-5).

Lasso 1592 *La fleur des chansons d'Orlande de Lassus, prince des musiciens de nostre temps. Contenant un recueil de ses chansons francoises, et italiennes, a quatre, cinc, six et huit parties accomodées tant aux instrumens comme a la voix, tout mises en ordre convenable selon leurs tons.* Antwerp: P. Phalèse and J. Bellère, 1592 (S-A-T-B-5-6); repr. 1596 (S-A-T-B-5-6), 1604 (S-A-T-B-5-6), 1612 (S-A-T-B), 1629 (5-6).

Lasso 1596 See Lasso 1592.

MANUSCRIPT SOURCE OF VOCAL COMPOSITIONS

WinF 153 Winchester College, Warden and Fellows' Library, MS. 153 ("Winchester Partbooks"). 1564–66.

PRINTED SOURCES OF INSTRUMENTAL COMPOSITIONS

Sigla for these sources identify the printer(s) or intabulator(s) and include label numbers from BrownIM.

Phal & Bell 1570[3] *Hortulus Cytharae, in Duos Distinctus Libros.* Antwerp: P. Phalèse and J. Bellère, 1570; repr. [1575][7].

Phal & Bell 1571[6] *Theatrum Musicum . . . Translata in Testudinis Usum, velut Julio Cesare Paduano, Melchiore Nenslyder [sic] Germano, & Sixto Kargl.* Louvain: P. Phalèse and J. Bellère, 1571.

Kargel 1574[1] *Novae, Elegantissimae, Gallicae, Item et Italicae Cantilenae . . . in Tabulaturam per M. Sixtum Kaergel Lautenistam.* Strasbourg: B. Jobin, 1574. Possible earlier edition [1569][4].

Kargel & Lais 1575[3] *Toppel Cythar . . . gestelt durch Sixtum Kärgel Lautenisten, und Johan Dominico Lais.* Strasbourg: B. Jobin, 1575; repr. 1578[5]. Possible first edition [1569][3].

Kargel 1578[4] *Renovata Cythara . . . durch Sixt Kärgel Lautenisten.* Strasbourg: B. Jobin, 1578; repr. 1580[2]. Possible earlier editions [1569][5] and [1575][2].

Kargel & Lais 1578[5] See 1575[3].

Kargel 1580[2] See 1578[4].

Phal & Bell 1582[5] *Hortulus Citharae . . . in Tabulaturam Citharae Convenienter Redacta.* Antwerp: P. Phalèse and J. Bellère, 1582.

Adriansen 1584[6] *Pratum Musicum . . . Omnia ad Testudinis Tabulaturam Fideliter Redacta, per id Genus Musices Experientissimum Artificem Emanuelem Hadrianium Antverpiensem.* Antwerp: P. Phalèse, 1584.

MANUSCRIPT SOURCE OF INSTRUMENTAL COMPOSITIONS

CoimU 242 Coimbra, Biblioteca Geral da Universidade, MS. 242 (ca. 1586).

LITERATURE CITED

Alta.D Altamura, Antonio. *Dizionario dialettale napoletano.* Naples: F. Fiorentino, 1956.

Bas.C Basile, Giambattista. *Lo cunto de li cunti.* Edited by Mario Petrini. Scrittori d'Italia, 260. Bari: G. Laterza, 1976.

Batt.G Battaglia, Salvatore. *Grande dizionario della lingua italiana.* 13 vols. Turin: Unione Tipografico-Editrice Torinese, 1961–.

Boett.OL Boetticher, Wolfgang. *Orlando di Lasso und seine Zeit, 1532–1594.* Kassel: Bärenreiter, 1958.

BrownIM Brown, Howard Mayer. *Instrumental Music Printed before 1600: A Bibliography.* Cambridge: Harvard University Press, 1967.

Card.CV Cardamone, Donna G. *The "Canzone villanesca alla napolitana" and Related Forms, 1537–1570.* 2 vols. Ann Arbor: UMI Research Press, 1981.

Cro.S Croce, Benedetto. *La Spagna nella vita italiana durante la rinascenza.* 2d ed. Bari: G. Laterza, 1922.

Ein.IM Einstein, Alfred. *The Italian Madrigal.* 3 vols. Princeton, N.J.: Princeton University Press, 1949.

Gal.V   Galanti, Bianca Maria. *Le villanelle alla napolitana.* Biblioteca dell'Archivum Romanicum, ser. 1, vol. 39. Florence: Leo S. Olschki, 1954.

LassoW   Lasso, Orlando di. *Sämtliche Werke.* Vol. 10, *Madrigale,* pt. 5. Edited by Adolf Sandberger. Leipzig: Breitkopf & Härtel, 1898.

Mal.P   Malato, Enrico. *La poesia dialettale napoletana.* 2 vols. Naples: Edizioni Scientifiche Italiane, 1960.

NolaO   Nola, Gian Domenico del Giovane da. *I documenti biografici e l'attività presso la SS. Annunziata con l'opera completa.* Edited by Lionello Cammarota. 2 vols. Rome: Edizioni De Santis, 1973.

Penz.P   Penzer, Norman M., ed. *The Pentamerone of Giambattista Basile.* 2 vols. London: John Lane, 1932.

Pra.V   Prati, Angelico. *Vocabolario etimologico italiano.* Milan: Garzanti, 1970.

RISM   *Répertoire international des sources musicales,* ser. B/1, *Recueils imprimés, XVIᵉ–XVIIᵉ siècles.* Munich-Duisberg: G. Henle Verlag, 1960.

Sper.P   Speroni, Charles. "Proverbs and Proverbial Phrases in Basile's 'Pentameron.'" *University of California Publications in Modern Philology* 24, no. 2 (1941): 181–288.

Torr.P   Torriano, Giovanni. *Piazza universale di proverbi italiani; or, A Commonplace of Italian Proverbs and Proverbial Phrases.* 3 vols. London: Printed by F. and T. W. for the author, 1666.

Villanesche from Lasso's "Opus I" (1555)

[1] *La cortesia voi donne predicate*

1. La cortesia voi[1] donne predicate,
   Ma mai non l'osservate, vi so dire.[2]
   > *Voi lo vedete[3] s'è come dico io,*
   > *Sol ch'io ti[4] parlo, dici, "va' con dio."[5]*

2. Se la dicete perchè non me amate,
   Et hai pietà di tanto mio martire.
   > *Voi lo vedete . . .*

3. Quando vi tengo mente,[6] ve n'entrate,
   E senza causa me voi far morire.
   > *Voi lo vedete . . .*

4. Va' figlia mia, ca[7] se voi predicare,
   L'opere bone ti bisogna fare.
   > *Voi lo vedete . . .*

1. You ladies preach courtesy
   But never observe it, I can assure you.
   > *You know it's just as I say it is,*
   > *Yet when I talk to you, you say, "Get lost."*

2. So you say that because you don't love me,
   And you pity my great suffering.
   > *You know . . .*

3. When I'm attentive to you, you come in,
   And for no reason you make me die.
   > *You know . . .*

4. Go, my girl, because if you want to preach,
   You must do good deeds.
   > *You know . . .*

SOURCE: RISM 1555¹⁹, fol. 11r.

CONCORDANCES: RISM 1555²⁹(S); [1558QL]; RISM 1560⁴; WinF 153, fol. 24v; Lasso 1565 (A-T-B), fol. 9v; Lasso 1567 (T-B), fol. 9v; Lasso 1570, fol. 9v; RISM 1570⁶, p. 4; Lasso 1584, fol. 10; Lasso 1596, fol. 12.

MODEL: Fontana 1545, no. 16 (see no. [7] in this edition).

NOTES ON THE TEXT: RISM 1555¹⁹, RISM 1555²⁹, [1558QL], RISM 1560⁴, WinF 153, Lasso 1565, Lasso 1567, Lasso 1570, and Lasso 1584 include four strophes. Refrain cues in strophes not underlaid to music are lacking in all sources; in Lasso 1584 the entire refrain is given once with strophe 2. RISM 1570⁶ and Lasso 1596 include but one strophe. Repeat symbols for text are used in all but three sources in accordance with RISM 1555¹⁹. In WinF 153, Lasso 1565, and Lasso 1567, repeated phrases are generally written out.

    1. "voi" is "noi" in Tenor, RISM 1555¹⁹.
    2. "dire" is "dice" in Tenor and Bassus, RISM 1560⁴.
    3. "vedete" is "vedere" in RISM 1555¹⁹. Corrected to "vedete" as in WinF 153 (Bassus) and all sources after 1567.
    4. "ti" is "ri" in Tenor, RISM 1560⁴.
    5. "dio" is "aio" in Bassus, RISM 1555¹⁹.

6. *tengo mente*, Neapolitan for *stare attento* (Bas.C, 726).

7. "ca" is "ta" in all parts, RISM 1560[4]; Neapolitan for *perchè*.

Notes on the Music: Mensuration sign is ¢ in RISM 1555[19], RISM 1555[29], [1558QL], RISM 1560[4], and WinF 153. It is ₵ in Lasso 1565, Lasso 1567, Lasso 1570, RISM 1570[6], Lasso 1584, and Lasso 1596.   M. 4, Contratenor, note 2, accidental lacking in RISM 1560[4].   Mm. 7 and 15, Tenor, note 1, e♭' in Lasso 1584 and Lasso 1596.   M. 17, Tenor, note 1, e♭' in Lasso 1596.   M. 21, Bassus, note 1, c in WinF 153.   M. 23, Tenor, note 1, e♭' in Lasso 1570, Lasso 1584, and Lasso 1596.   M. 24, Tenor, note 2, e♭' in Lasso 1584 and Lasso 1596.   M. 35, Superius, note 2, accidental lacking in RISM 1560[4] and Lasso 1584, note 4 has sharp in Lasso 1570.

[2] *Madonna mia, pietà chiam'et aita*

1. Madonna mia, pietà chiam'et aita,[1]
   Ch'io moro e stento a[2] torto, e pur volete.

   Io grido e nol sentete,
   "Acqua madonna[3] al foco,[4]
   Ch'io mi sento morire, a poco a poco."

2. Vostra altiera beltà, sola infinita,
   È causa ch'io me abbruscia,[5] e 'l consentete.

   Io grido . . .

3. Hormai le scema l'affanata vita,
   Nol credi, e con vostri occhi[6] lo vedete.

   Io grido . . .

4. Di chiedervi mercé son quasi roco,
   Sol della pena mia prendete gioco.

   Pur grido in ogni loco,
   "Acqua madonna al foco,
   Ch'io mi sento morire, a poco a poco."

1. My lady, I'm calling for mercy and help,
   Because I'm wrongfully half-starved, yet you allow it.

   I cry out and you don't listen,
   "Water the fire, lady,
   For I feel myself dying, little by little."

2. Your lofty beauty, unique and boundless,
   Is what causes me to scorch, and you permit it.

   I cry out . . .

3. Now my troubled life is waning;
   You don't believe it, yet with your eyes you see it.

   I cry out . . .

4. I'm nearly hoarse begging for your mercy,
   Only you make fun of my suffering.

   Still I cry out wherever I go,
   "Water the fire, lady,
   For I feel myself dying, little by little."

Source: RISM 1555[19], fol. 9v.

Concordances: RISM 1555[29](S); [1558QL]; RISM 1560[4]; WinF 153, fol. 22v; Lasso 1565 (A-T-B), fol. 6v; Lasso 1567 (T-B), fol. 6v; Lasso 1570, fol. 6v; RISM 1570[6], p. 1; Lasso 1584, fol. 8v; Lasso 1596, fol. 10v.

Model: Fontana 1545, no. 8 (see no. [8] in this edition).

Notes on the Text: RISM 1555[19], RISM 1555[29], [1558QL], RISM 1560[4], WinF 153, Lasso 1565, Lasso 1567, Lasso 1570, and Lasso 1584 include four strophes. Only Lasso 1584 has refrain cues in strophes not underlaid to the music. RISM 1570[6] and Lasso 1596 include but one strophe. Repeat symbols for text are used in all but one source in accordance with RISM 1555[19]. In WinF 153 repeated phrases are generally written out.

1. "aita" is "aito" in Tenor, RISM 1560[4].

2. "stento a" is "stent'a" in Contratenor, RISM 1555[19]; "stent'o a" in Tenor, RISM 1555[19], and in all parts, RISM 1560[4].

3. "madonna" is "madona" in Superius, Contratenor, and Tenor, RISM 1555[19], and Superius, RISM 1555[29].

4. "al foco" is "a foco" in all parts, RISM 1560[4].

5. *abbruscia*, Neapolitan for *bruciare, abrosciare*.

6. "occhi" is "acchi" in all parts, RISM 1560[4].

Madonna mia, pietà originated in Fontana's book of 1545 (see no. [8]). Almost all the salient conceits in *Madonna mia, pietà* are concentrated in the first strophe of another *villanesca* in Fontana's book:

> 1. Io grido sempre, hayme, non son inteso,
>   E di chiamar mercé son fatto roco.
>   *Acqua madonna al foco,*
>   *Ch'abruscio dentr'e tu te 'l prend'in gioco.*

The relationship between the poems is the result of verbal parody, not unusual in the *villanesca* repertory at this time (see Card.CV, 1:209–22). It is difficult to determine which poem served as the source for material they have in common. Fontana may have been the author of both poems, since many *villanesca* composers

xxxix

of his generation provided their own *poesia per musica*. The transmission history shows that the poems were well known in northern circles. Antonio Barges, a Netherlander who resided in Venice, reworked Fontana's three-voice settings of *Madonna mia, pietà* and *Io grido sempre* for four voices and printed them in successive order in his book *Il primo libro de villotte a quatro voci* (Venice: A. Gardane, 1550), 1 and 2. A slightly different version of *Io grido sempre* circulated in a miscellany of popular poetry printed in Venice by Mattio Pagan: *Nove canzone napolitane sopra vari propositi*, fol. 3v (exemplar in London, British Library, 1071.c.65/12). This book is not dated, but it would have been printed sometime between 1543 and 1557 when Pagan was active in Venice. Pagan evidently derived *Io grido sempre* from a musical source, either oral or written, for he reproduced the verse lines as they might have been repeated or truncated when sung in the Neapolitan manner:

> 1. Io grido sempre, io grido sempre mai,
>   Ma non son inteso.
>   E de chiamar mercé son fatto roco.
>   *Aqua madonna al foco, aqua madonna al foco,*
>   *Ch'abruscio dentro e tu lo metti in gioco.*

Variants within and between settings of *Madonna mia, pietà* and *Io grido sempre* reflect the comparative freedom with which poets used and recombined memorable phrases from the current fund of popular verse, guided by their ear for the patterns of vernacular speech. An example of this approach is found in a *moresca* by Lasso, *Hai Lucia bona cosa* (Lasso 1581, fol. 5v, and LassoW, 86), where a popular song is quoted in response to the line "gente negra vol cantare." It is a cento of lines from *Madonna mia, pietà* and *Io grido sempre* and may have been created by Lasso himself:

Acqua madonna al fuoco,	Lady, water the fire,
Che ardo tutto e tu pigliat'a gioco.	Because I'm burning up and you make fun of me.
Io grido sempre, haime, et tu non sentuta,	I continue to cry out, alas, but you don't hear me,
Et voce mia tutto fatta roca.	And my voice has grown quite hoarse.
Acqua madonna al fuoco che ci minera,	Lady, water the fire that pains me,
Ard'e mo fuiuta cocha.	I'm burning and now the cook has fled.

NOTES ON THE MUSIC: Mensuration sign is C in RISM 1555[19], RISM 1555[29], [1558QL], RISM 1560[4], and WinF 153. It is ¢ in Lasso 1565, Lasso 1567, Lasso 1570, RISM 1570[6], Lasso 1584, and Lasso 1596.   Mm. 2 and 7, Superius, note 2, no accidental after rest.   M. 22, Superius, note 3, accidental lacking in WinF 153.   M. 26, Bassus, note 5, accidental lacking in Lasso 1584.   M. 29, Tenor, note 2, c♯' in Lasso 1565.   M. 33, Bassus, note 5, accidental lacking in Lasso 1584.   M. 34, Tenor, note 2, accidental lacking in WinF 153.

Barges's arrangement of *Madonna mia, pietà* (source noted above) bears no relationship to Lasso's other than the use of the same tune in the Tenor borrowed from Fontana (see Card.CV, vol. 2, no. 10).

[3] *'No giorno t'haggio havere intra 'ste mane*

1. 'No[1] giorno t'haggio havere[2] intra 'ste mane, 　Se 'nce[3] dovesse perdere le zappe.[4] 　*Fugimi quanto voi, che non mi scappi.[5]*	1. Some day I shall catch hold of you, 　Even if I should ruin my hoes. 　*Run away as much as you want, for you can't escape me.*
2. Non ce pensare, no, lascia 'se[6] trame, 　Si' 'ngi[7] sentita e fa che non ce 'ncappi.[8] 　*Fugimi . . .*	2. Don't consider it, don't, give up all your tricks, 　Mind you, don't get caught up in it. 　*Run away . . .*
3. Me stratii[9] e me beffeggi come cane, 　Et io, papieto,[10] 'nce stongo[11] a 'se mappi. 　*Fugimi . . .*	3. You torture me and tease me like a dog, 　And I, greedy old man, put up with all your schemes. 　*Run away . . .*
4. Dove va trenta, ben può ir[12] trenta uno,[13] 　Ch'io t'aggio haver al dispetto d'ognuno. 　*Fugimi . . .*	4. Where there's room for thirty, one more can go, 　For I shall get hold of you despite everyone. 　*Run away . . .*

SOURCE: RISM 1555[19], fol. 10v.

CONCORDANCES: RISM 1555[29] (S); [1558QL]; RISM 1560[4]; Lasso 1565 (A-T-B), fol. 8v; Lasso 1567 (T-B), fol. 8v; Lasso 1570, fol. 8v; RISM 1570[6], p. 3; Lasso 1584, fol. 9v; and Lasso 1596, fol. 11v.

MODEL: Fontana 1545, no. 6 (see no. [9] in this edition).

NOTES ON THE TEXT: RISM 1555[19], RISM 1555[29], [1558QL], RISM 1560[4], Lasso 1565, Lasso 1567, Lasso 1570, and Lasso 1584 include four strophes. Only in Lasso 1584 is the refrain line given after each couplet. RISM 1570[6] and Lasso 1596 include but one strophe.

1. 'No, Neapolitan for *uno*.

2. "havere" is "haver" in Contratenor, RISM 1555[19].

3. 'nce, Neapolitan for *non ci*.

4. *zappe*—In some regions of southern Italy (Avezzano, for example), *zappa* means goat because of the resemblance of a *zappa-bidente* (two-pronged fork) to goat horns (Pra.V, 1060). Armed with such "weapons," the frustrated lover chases the object of his rude desire as if she were a stray animal, determined to dig into her even if he should lose everything.

5. The entire refrain line is the first line of an anonymous *villanesca* in *Elletione de canzone alla napoletana a tre voci di Rinaldo Burno con altre scielte da diverse musici* ([Padua: Fabriano and Bindoni?,] 1546), 3.

6. 'se (alt. sp. of 'sse), Neapolitan for *coteste*; see also strophe 3, line 2.

7. Si' (alt. sp. of *sia, sie*) 'ngi (alt. sp. of *nge, nce*).

8. 'ncappi, Neapolitan for *incappiare*.

9. "stratii" is "straty" in all parts, RISM 1555[19], RISM 1555[29], [1558QL], and RISM 1560[4].

10. *papieto*, diminutive of *Pappo*, old blockhead or clodhopper, a comic type that originated in Atellan farce. The mask Pappus was not only a glutton but lustful as well—a contradiction of senility. The aging pursuer in this poem appears all the more ridiculous because of his vigorous threats.

11. *stongo* (alt. sp. of *sto*), Neapolitan.

12. *ir* (alt. sp. of *ire*), Neapolitan for *andare*.

13. This line is an allusion to the *trentuno*, a degrading form of revenge practiced on traitorous courtesans, so-called because the unfortunate woman was sequestered and raped by thirty-one men. See the prologue of Francesco Belo's *Il pedante* (1529) and Lorenzo Venier's notorious poem "Il trentuno di Zaffetta," in which the *trentuno reale* (rape by seventy-nine men) was inflicted on a Venetian courtesan who failed to ask permission of a regular client to entertain another. Torriano was more discreet in his description of the *trentuno*: "To work one's revenge upon Bawds and Whores, after having been abus'd and trapann'd by them; and this punishment by having one and thirty blows or lashes at them by so many several persons appointed, or if not by so many, so often repeated as to make up the number" (Torr.P, 2:221).

NOTES ON THE MUSIC: Mensuration sign is 𝄴 in RISM 1555[19], RISM 1555[29], [1558QL], and RISM 1560[4]. It is 𝄵 in Lasso 1565, Lasso 1567, Lasso 1570, RISM 1570[6], Lasso 1584, and Lasso 1596. The proportion at mm. 19 and 25 is denoted by coloration and by the numeral 3 positioned on the staff directly before each group of three notes in all sources except Lasso 1584. The return to *integer valor* at mm. 22 and 28 is indicated by 𝄵 in Lasso 1565, Lasso 1567, Lasso 1570 (m. 28, Tenor, 3 given erroneously), and Lasso 1596. The same proportion in Lasso 1584 is denoted by a single numeral 3, the return to *integer valor* by 𝄵. M. 15, Contratenor, note 2, accidental lacking in Lasso 1565 and Lasso 1584.

[4] *'Sto core mio se fosse di diamante*

1. 'Sto core mio se fosse di diamante,
   Saria spezzato per tanto dolore,
      Quanto ne provo e[1] sent'a tutte l'hore.

2. Et ben ch'afflitto sia più ch'altro amante,
   Tenga dolente e sconsolato il core,
      Pur non li manca spirto nè vigore.

3. Ma quanto più patisce[2] e più constante,
   Sofre il dolor se ben fosse[3] magiore,
      Di quel ch'io provo e sento a tutte l'hore.

4. Ma voi, donna crudel, volete anchora,
   Per magior[4] segno di mia fede ogn'hora,
      Vedermi tormentar prima ch'io mora.

1. Even if my heart were made of diamond,
   It would splinter from the sharp pain
      That I feel and sense hour by hour.

2. Although I'm afflicted more than other lovers,
   My heart discouraged and reduced to sorrow,
      Nonetheless it lacks neither strength nor spirit.

3. But however much it suffers and how steadily,
   It would gladly bear a greater pain
      Than what I feel and sense hour by hour.

4. But you, cruel lady, never satisfied,
   Demand still greater proof of my devotion,
      To torture me until I die.

Source: RISM 1555[19], fol. 12r.

Concordances: RISM 1555[29] (S); [1558QL]; RISM 1560[4]; WinF 153, fol. 26; Lasso 1565 (A-T-B), fol. 11; Lasso 1567 (T-B), fol. 11; Lasso 1570, fol. 11; RISM 1570[6], p. 6; Lasso 1584, fol. 11; and Lasso 1596, fol. 13.

Model: RISM 1565[11], p. 10 (anon.; see no. [10] in this edition).

Notes on the Text: RISM 1555[19], RISM 1555[29], [1558QL], RISM 1560[4], WinF 153, Lasso 1565, Lasso 1567, Lasso 1570, and Lasso 1584 include four strophes. In Lasso 1584 there are four residual strophes instead of three due to a redundant insertion of line 3 from strophe 1. RISM 1570[6] and Lasso 1596 include but one strophe. Repeat symbols for text are used in all but four sources in accordance with RISM 1555[19]. In WinF 153, Lasso 1565, Lasso 1567, and Lasso 1570, repeated phrases are generally written out.

    1. "provo e" is "prov'et" in Superius, RISM 1555[19] and RISM 1555[29]; "provo prov'es" in Superius, RISM 1560[4].

    2. "patisce" is "patiesce" in all parts, RISM 1560[4].

    3. "fosse" is "forsse" in Superius, RISM 1555[19], RISM 1555[29], and WinF 153.

    4. "magior" is "maior" in all parts, RISM 1560[4].

Notes on the Music: Mensuration sign is C in RISM 1555[19], RISM 1555[29], [1558QL], RISM 1560[4], and WinF 153. It is ¢ in Lasso 1565, Lasso 1567, Lasso 1570, RISM 1570[6], Lasso 1584, and Lasso 1596. Key signature is two B-flats in Contratenor and Bassus of RISM 1555[19], [1558QL], RISM 1560[4], WinF 153, and Lasso 1584, and one flat in all other sources. Mm. 1 and 6, Superius, note 1, accidental lacking in Lasso 1570 and Lasso 1584. M. 23, Superius, note 3 has sharp in WinF 153. M. 24, Superius, note 2 has sharp in WinF 153; Contratenor, note 2, e' in Lasso 1570 and Lasso 1584; Tenor, note 2, c' in Lasso 1570 and Lasso 1584.

[5] *Tu sai, madonna mia, ch'io t'amo et voglio*

1. Tu sai, madonna mia, ch'io t'amo[1] et voglio
   Tanto di ben ch'io non ritrovo loco.
     Perchè prendete'l mio martir in gioco?[2]

2. Se sai che del tuo laccio mai mi scioglio,
   Et per voi me nutrico in fiamma e foco,
     Perchè . . .

3. Se sai che la mia fede è fermo scoglio,
   Che per voi mi consumo, a poco a poco,
     Perchè . . .

4. Dunque madonna, cessa il tuo furore,
   Habbi pietà di chi t'a dato il core,
     Ch'in vita e morte t'è bon servitore.

1. You know, my lady, that I love and desire you
   So much I can't find a comfortable place.
     Why do you make fun of my torment?

2. If you know I'll never slip out of your noose,
   And I'm nourished in your fire and passion,
     Why . . .

3. If you know that my faith is steady as a rock,
   That for you I melt away, little by little,
     Why . . .

4. So lady, stop your raging,
   Take pity on one who has given you his heart,
     And who in life and death is your good servant.

Source: RISM 1555[19], fol. 10r.

Concordances: RISM 1555[29] (S); [1558QL]; RISM 1560[4]; WinF 153, fol. 23v; Lasso 1565 (A-T-B), fol. 7v; Lasso 1567 (T-B), fol. 7v; Lasso 1570, fol. 7v; RISM 1570[6], p. 2; Lasso 1584, fol. 9; Lasso 1596, fol. 11.

Model: Fontana 1545, no. 4 (see no. [11] in this edition).

Notes on the Text: RISM 1555[19], RISM 1555[29], [1558QL], RISM 1560[4], WinF 153, Lasso 1565, Lasso 1567, Lasso 1570, and Lasso 1584 include four strophes. Only Lasso 1584 has refrain cues in strophes not underlaid to the music. RISM 1570[6] and Lasso 1596 include but one strophe. Repeat symbols for text are used in all but two sources in accordance with RISM 1555[19]. In WinF 153 and Lasso 1565, repeated phrases are written out.

    1. "t'amo" is "ta'mo" in Superius, RISM 1555[19] and RISM 1555[29].

    2. "gioco" is "gioto" in Bassus, RISM 1560[4].

Notes on the Music: Mensuration sign is C in RISM 1555[19], RISM 1555[29], [1558QL], RISM 1560[4], and WinF 153. It is ¢ in Lasso 1565, Lasso 1567, Lasso 1570, RISM 1570[6], Lasso 1584, and Lasso 1596. Key signature is two B-flats in Bassus of RISM 1555[19], [1558QL], RISM 1560[4], and WinF 153, and one flat in all other sources. M. 9, Bassus, note 2, accidental lacking in Lasso 1584.

[6] *Tu, traditora, m'hai puost'a 'sto core*

1. Tu, traditora, m'hai puost'a[1] 'sto core,
   'No focolaro di fiamma[2] e di foco.
   E mo canazza,[3] me la mietti in gioco.

2. Et ence[4] tanta[5] brascia[6] e tanto ardore,
   Ch'uno acino di miglio non ce ha luoco.
   E mo . . .

3. E sentoci quello asino d'amore,[7]
   Che sempre atizza[8] come fosse cuoco.
   E mo . . .

4. Provedeci ti dico, e non tardare,
   Ca[9] non è cosa da chiù comportare.
   Farmi senza proposito abrusciare.[10]

1. You, traitor, have hatched in my heart
   A hotbed of flame and fire.
   And now, cruel mistress, you make fun of me.

2. There is so much glowing and burning
   That not even a kernel of birdseed can exist in it.
   And now . . .

3. I feel that jackass Cupid here,
   Who forever fans the fire as if he were a cook.
   And now . . .

4. Take care of it I tell you, and don't delay,
   Because it's not something to tolerate any longer.
   Make me scorch to no purpose.

SOURCE: RISM 1555[19], fol. 11v.

CONCORDANCES: RISM 1555[29] (S); [1558QL]; RISM 1560[4]; WinF 153, fol. 25v; Lasso 1565 (A-T-B), fol. 10v; Lasso 1567 (T-B), fol. 10v; Lasso 1570, fol. 10v; RISM 1570[6], p. 5; Lasso 1584, fol. 10v; Lasso 1596, fol. 12v.

NOTES ON THE TEXT: RISM 1555[19], RISM 1555[29], [1558QL], RISM 1560[4], WinF 153, Lasso 1565, Lasso 1567, Lasso 1570, and Lasso 1584 include four strophes. Only Lasso 1584 has refrain cues in strophes not underlaid to the music. RISM 1570[6] and Lasso 1596 include but one strophe. Repeat symbols for text are generally used in all sources in accordance with RISM 1555[19].

  1. *puost'a,* from *porre,* used here in the sense of *covare* (Pra.V, 789).
  2. "di fiamma" is "de fiamma" in Superius, RISM 1555[19], RISM 1555[29], [1558QL], and RISM 1560[4].
  3. *canazza,* Neapolitan for *amata crudele* (Bas.C, 700).
  4. *ence,* Neapolitan for *ce n'è.*
  5. "tanta" is "tanat" in all parts, RISM 1560[4].
  6. *brascia,* old form of brace, literally smoldering embers (Pra.V, 161).
  7. "amore" is "amere" in all parts, RISM 1560[4].
  8. *atizza*—The figurative meaning is *incitare.*
  9. *ca,* Neapolitan for *perchè.*
  10. *abrusciare,* Neapolitan for *bruciare* or *abrosciare.*

Three other readings of *Tu, traditora* are extant. The one in Dorico's Roman anthology of *villanelle* (RISM 1555[30]) resembles Susato's most closely; the words that differ do not alter the meaning:

1. Tu, traditora, m'hai post'a 'sto core,
   'No focolaro di fum'e di foco.
   E mo canaza, me la miet'a gioco.

2. Et ence tanta fiam'et tant'ardore,
   Che n'acino di miglio non c'ha luoco.
   E mo . . .

3. Et sentoce quell'aseno d'amore,
   Che sempre attizza come fusse cuoco.
   E mo . . .

4. Provedence cor mio, et non tardare,
   Ca non è cosa da se comportare.
   Farmi senza proposito abrusciare.

A version of *Tu, traditora* containing variants from the Veneto region circulated in a miscellany printed in Venice by Mattio Pagan: *Nove canzone napolitane sopra vari propositi,* fol. 2v (see also "Notes on the Text," no. [2]).

1. Tu, traditora, m'ai posto a 'sto core,
   Un fogolaro de fiama e de foco.
   E me, de mo canaza,
   E mo canaza, me la mete in gioco.

2. Et hagio tanta fiamma e tanto ardore,
   Che un agelo di miglio non chi a loco.
   E me . . .

3. E deta chi è quel asinel d'amore,
   Che sempre tiza come fusi quoco.
   E me . . .

4. Providimi te dico, e non tardare,
   Che non è cosa de lo comportare.
   Farme senza proposito,
   Farme senza proposito abrusiare.

The version of *Tu, traditora* that least resembles Susato's reading is located in a miscellany of popular poetry of unknown date and provenance: *Opera nuova dove si contiene molte belle vilanelle napolitane,* fol. 3r (Gal.V, 105). In addition to minor spelling variants and printing errors, major differences characterize this reading: inversion of strophes 2 and 3, a new refrain line in strophe 4, and the substitution of "piglie" for "mietti" in strophe 1.

NOTES ON THE MUSIC: Mensuration sign is ₵ in RISM 1555[19], RISM 1555[29], [1558QL], RISM 1560[4], and WinF 153. It is ₵ in Lasso 1565, Lasso 1567, Lasso 1570, RISM 1570[6], Lasso 1584, and Lasso 1596. M. 1, Superius, upbeat, accidental lacking in Lasso 1570 and Lasso 1584. M. 12, Contratenor, notes 2–3, dotted croma, semiminim in RISM 1555[19], [1558QL], RISM 1560[4], and RISM 1570[6]. M. 14, Bassus, note 1, accidental lacking in RISM 1570[6]. Mm. 14 and 20, Contratenor, note 1, lacking dot in Lasso 1596, notes 2–3, crome in RISM 1570[6] and Lasso 1596.

Only the Superius and Tenor are extant from the three-part setting of *Tu, traditora* published in Rome by Dorico: RISM 1555[30], no. 19 (S); repr. 1558[16] (T). Lasso's name figures prominently in the title of Dorico's anthology, but no attributions are given within. Einstein believes that all the *villanelle* were anonymous and that Lasso's name was used solely for promotional reasons (Ein.IM, 2:497). Boetticher argues that Lasso composed the three-part setting, which then served as model for his arrangement (Boett.OL, 42). If this were the case, then Lasso or Susato made the changes in the poem. The Superius of the three-part setting is given below. (The Tenor partbook from the 1558 reprint could not be consulted.)

RISM 1555[30]
Anon.

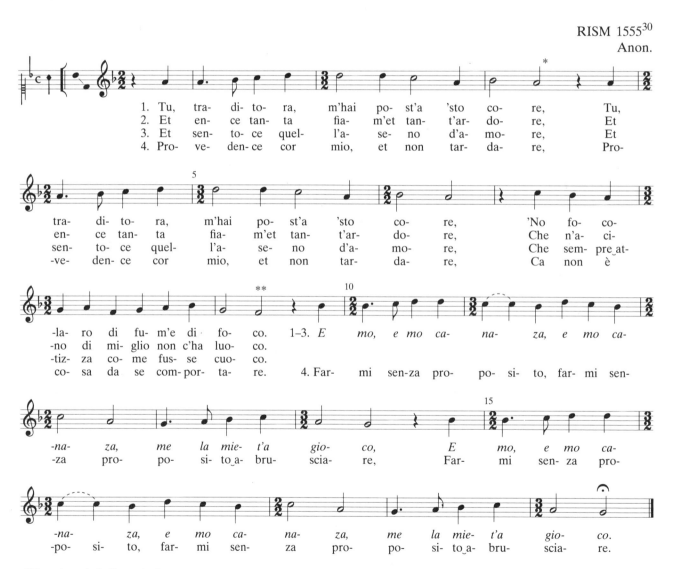

*Repeat symbol after note 2.

**A vertical bar after note 2 limits the extent of the repetition prescribed by a repeat symbol followed by a second ending at the close of the final strain.

Neapolitan Models for Lasso's *Villanesche*

[7] *La cortesia voi donne predicate (Fontana)*

1. La cortesia voi donne predicate,
   Ma mai non l'osservate, vi so dire.
   > Voi lo vedete[1] s'è come dico io,
   > Sol ch'io ti parlo, dici, "va' con dio."

2. Se la dicete perchè non me amate,
   Et hai pietà di tanto mio martire.
   > Voi lo vedete . . .

3. Quando ve tengo mente, ve n'entrate,
   E senza causa me voi far morire.
   > Voi lo vedete . . .

4. Va' figlia mia, ca se voi predicare,
   L'opere bone ti bisogna fare.
   > Voi lo vedete . . .

SOURCE: Fontana 1545, no. 16 (unicum).

NOTES ON THE TEXT: For the annotated text and translation, see no. [1].
   1. "vedete" is "vedere" in all parts.

NOTES ON THE MUSIC: No errors.

For a vihuela intabulation, see *Libro de musica de vihuela, agora nuevamente compuesto por Diego Pisador* (Salamanca: D. Pisador, 1552), bk. 7, fol. 88r.

[8] *Madonna mia, pietà chiam'et aita (Fontana)*

1. Madonna mia, pietà chiam'et aita,
   Ch'io moro e stento a torto pur volete.
   > Io grido e nol sentete,
   > "Acqua madonn'al foco,
   > Ch'io mi sento morire, a poco a poco."

2. Vostra altiera beltà, sola infinita,
   Gli è causa ch'io me abbruscia, e 'l consentete.
   > Pur grido . . .

3. Hormai le scema l'affanata vita,
   Nol credi, e con vostri occhi lo vedete.
   > Pur grido . . .

4. Di chiedervi mercé son quasi roco,
   Sol della pena mia prendete gioco.
   > Pur grido in ogni loco,
   > "Acqua madonn'al foco,
   > Ch'io mi sento morire, a poco a poco."

SOURCE: Fontana 1545, no. 8 (unicum).

NOTES ON THE TEXT: For the annotated text and translation, see no. [2].

NOTES ON THE MUSIC: No errors.

[9] *'No giorno t'hagio havere intra 'ste mane (Fontana)*

1. 'No giorno t'hagio havere intra 'ste mane,
   Se 'nce dovesse perdere le zappe.
   > Fuggimi quanto voi, che non mi scappi.

2. Non ce pensare, no, lascia 'se trame,
   Si' 'ngi sentita e fa che no ce 'ncapi.[1]
   > Fuggimi . . .

3. Me stratii[2] e me beffeggi come cane,
   E io, papieto, 'nce stongo a 'se mape.
   > Fuggimi . . .

4. Dove va trenta, ben può ir trenta uno,
   Ch'io t'haggio haver a dispetto d'ognuno.
   > Fuggimi . . .

SOURCE: Fontana 1545, no. 6 (unicum).

NOTES ON THE TEXT: For the annotated text and translation, see no. [3].
   1. "ce 'ncapi" is "ce'n capi" in all parts.
   2. "stratii" is "strati" in all parts.

NOTES ON THE MUSIC: Mm. 21 and 27, the return to *integer valor* is not indicated.

[10] *'Sto core mio se fusse de diamante (Anon.)*

1. 'Sto core mio se fusse de diamante,
   Saria spezzato per tanto dolore,
   > Quanto ne prov'e sent'a tutte l'hore.

2. E ben ch'afflitto sia più ch'altr'amante,[1]
   Et mesto sia[2] et sconsolato il cuore,
   > Non le mancha nè forza nè vigore.[3]

3. Ma quanto più patisc'e più costante,
   Sta nel martir[4] se[5] ben fosse maggiore,
   Di quel ch'io sento et prov'a tutte l'hore.

4. Et voi, donna crudel, volete anchora,
   Per maggior pena[6] di mia fed'ogn'hora,
   Vedermi tormentar[7] prima ch'io mora.

SOURCE: RISM 1565[11], p. 10.

CONCORDANCES: RISM 1560[12] (C-T), p. 17; and RISM 1571[5], p. 17.

NOTES ON THE TEXT: For the translation, see no. [4].
   1. "ch'altr'amante" is "ch'altramente" in all parts, RISM 1560[12] and RISM 1571[5].
   2. In Lasso's text (no. [4]), the words "tenga dolente" occur in place of "et mesto sia."
   3. In Lasso's text (no. [4]), this line reads, "Pur non li manca spirto nè vigore."
   4. In Lasso's text (no. [4]), the words "sofre il dolor" occur in place of "sta nel martir."
   5. "se" is "e" in all parts, RISM 1565[11].
   6. In Lasso's text (no. [4]), the words "per magior segno" occur in place of "per maggior pena."
   7. "tormentar" is "tormenta" in all parts, RISM 1565[11].

NOTES ON THE MUSIC: No errors in RISM 1565[11], RISM 1560[12], and RISM 1571[5].   M. 5, repeat symbol after note 2 in all sources.

[11] *Tu sai, madonna mia, ch'io t'amo e voglio (Fontana)*

1. Tu sai, madonna mia, ch'io t'amo e voglio
   Tanto di ben ch'io non ritrovo[1] loco.
   Perchè prendete 'l mio martir in gioco?

2. Se sai che del tuo laccio mai mi scioglio,
   E per voi me nutrico in fiamma e foco.
   Perchè . . .

3. Se sai che la mia fed'è fermo scoglio,
   Che per voi mi[2] consumo, a poco a poco.
   Perchè . . .

4. Donche madonna, cessa il tuo furore,
   Habbi pietà di chi t'a datto il core.
   Ch'in vita e morte t'è bon servidore.[3]

SOURCE: Fontana 1545, no. 4 (unicum).

NOTES ON THE TEXT: For the translation, see no. [5]. An alternative to the text underlay in the Bassus, mm. 5–10 and 16–21, would be to retext the phrase as given in the Tenor.
   1. "ritrovo" is "trovo" in all parts—corrected to "ritrovo" by analogy with Lasso's text (no. [5]), which regularizes Fontana's ten-syllable line to eleven syllables.
   2. "mi" is "vi" in all parts—corrected to "mi" by analogy with Lasso's text (no. [5]).
   3. The refrain cue (as in strophes 2 and 3) is added erroneously after this line, which, although it is not a textual refrain, is to be sung to the music of the refrain, including the repeat.

NOTES ON THE MUSIC: No errors.

Villanelle from Lasso's *Libro de villanelle* (1581)

[12] *Ad altre le voi dare 'ste passate*

Ad altre le voi dare 'ste passate,
Che non che no[1] che voglio lo cocucco.
   La triche triche trac e trucco,[2]
   Ch'altro sta dentr'et io di fuor allucco.

SOURCE: Lasso 1581, fol. 3r.

CONCORDANCE: Lasso 1582, fol. 3r.

MODEL: Nola 1545(2), no. 12 (see no. [24] in this edition).

NOTES ON THE TEXT: For the annotated text and translation, see no. [24]. Lasso 1581 and Lasso 1582 include but one strophe; the model by Nola includes four strophes.
   1. "Che non che no" is "Che non con no" in Nola 1545(2).
   2. "La triche triche trac e trucco" is "La trich'e trach'e trucco" in Nola 1545(2).

NOTES ON THE MUSIC: M. 25, Alto, note 2, semiminim in Lasso 1582; Alto and Tenore, a double barline after "trucco" marks a division between refrain lines in Lasso 1581 and Lasso 1582—double barline lacking in Canto and Basso.

Another four-part setting of the same poem, attributed to Hubert Waelrant (although not included in printed collections of his secular works), may be found in WinF 153, fols. 65v–66r. Nola's *villanesca* also served as a model for Waelrant, who, like Lasso, included only the first strophe. Waelrant preserved a more literal relationship to the model than Lasso, quoting Nola's cantus and tenor almost verbatim and exchanging their positions in the texture.

[13] *Ecco la nimph'Ebrayca chiamata*

Ecco la nimph'Ebrayca[1] chiamata,
Più brutt'assai di Menech'e di Chiara.

   Lingite, pingite, stringite,
   Olà, mandragola scioffata,
   Che te ne vidi ca si' 'namorata.

SOURCE: Lasso 1581, fol. 2v.

CONCORDANCE: Lasso 1582, fol. 1v.

MODEL: Nola 1545(1), no. 17 (see no. [25] in this edition).

NOTES ON THE TEXT: For the annotated text and translation, see no. [25]. Lasso 1581 and Lasso 1582 include but one strophe; the model by Nola includes four strophes.
   1. "Ebrayca" is "ebrayca" in all parts, Lasso 1581 and Lasso 1582.

NOTES ON THE MUSIC: M. 29, Tenore, accidental before note 2 in Lasso 1581 and Lasso 1582.

[14] *Io ti voria contar la pena mia*

Io ti voria contar[1] la pena mia,
Ma non ce bastariano mille mesi.

   Ti dico, "voi me bene?"
   Tu mi rispondi, "sì."
   Dico, "fa'[2] questo mo."[3]
   Tu dici, "non si può."

SOURCE: Lasso 1581, fol. 5r.

CONCORDANCE: Lasso 1582, fol. 6v.

NOTES ON THE TEXT: Lasso 1581 and Lasso 1582 include but one strophe.   M. 7, Tenore, "io" included under the repeat symbol, Lasso 1582.
   1. "contar" is "cantar" in Tenore, Lasso 1582.
   2. "fa' " is "fà" in all parts, Lasso 1581 and Lasso 1582.
   3. "mo" is "mò" in all parts, Lasso 1581 and Lasso 1582.

The complete poem of four strophes is located in Fontana 1545, no. 18:

1. Io ti vorria contar la pena mia,
   Ma non ce bastariano mille mesi.
      Ti dico, "voi me bene?"
      Tu mi rispondi, "sì."
      Dico, "fa' questo mo."
      Tu dici, "non si può."

2. Trista et afflitta questa anima mia,
   Perchè non hagio scuti[a] nè tornesi.[b]
      Ti dico . . .

3. Fata ho la scorta e posta hagio la spia,
   Tutta tu si'[c] di principi e marchesi.

      Ti dico . . .

1. I would like to tell you of my pain,
   But a thousand months would not be long enough.
      I say to you, "Do you care about me?"
      You reply, "Yes."
      I say, "Do it now."
      You say, "It's not allowed."

2. Gloomy and depressed is my spirit,
   Because I have no money.
      I say to you . . .

3. I had you followed, and I sent a spy;
   You are totally preoccupied with princes and marchesi.

      I say to you . . .

<table>
<tr><td>4. A me mi par cha mi voi dar passate,
Mo mi parto da voi, adio siate.
   Ti dico . . .</td><td>4. To me it seems that you want to get rid of me;
Now I'll leave you, good-bye.
   I say to you . . .</td></tr>
</table>

    [a]*scuti* (alt. sp. of *scudi*), gold or silver coins bearing the figure of a shield.
    [b]*tornesi*, a coin first issued in Tours and subsequently used in Italy but given different values. In the kingdom of Naples its value was two *centesimi*, that is, worth very little.
    [c]*si'*, Neapolitan for *sei*.

NOTES ON THE MUSIC: Key signature is one B-flat in Basso of Lasso 1582.   Mm. 18 and 27, Tenore, accidental before note 3 in Lasso 1581 and Lasso 1582.
    The source of Lasso's model is unknown. For an edition of Fontana's setting, see Card.CV, vol. 2, no. 7.

[15] *O belle, fusa! chi ne vo' accatare?*

O belle, fusa! chi ne vo'[1] accatare?[2]
Noi le vendimo queste fus'in prova.
   Son fusa nova,
   Voi le provare?
   Venitell'a pigliare,
   Le dam'in prova.

SOURCE: Lasso 1581, fol. 6v.

CONCORDANCE: Lasso 1582, fol. 7r.

MODEL: Nola 1545(1), no. 13 (see no. [26] in this edition).

NOTES ON THE TEXT: For the annotated text and translation, see no. [26]. Lasso 1581 and Lasso 1582 have one strophe; the model by Nola has four strophes. The repeat of verse lines 4–6 is written out in Canto of Lasso 1581 and Lasso 1582, but not in the other parts.
    1. *vo'*, Neapolitan for *vuole*.
    2. "accatare" is "acatare" in Canto and Alto, Lasso 1581 and Lasso 1582.

NOTES ON THE MUSIC: No errors.

[16] *O occhi manza mia, cigli dorati*

O occhi manza mia, cigli dorati,
O faccia d'una luna stralucenti.[1]
   Tienemi mente,[2]
   Gioia mia bella,
   Guardam'un poc'a me, fami contiento.[3]

SOURCE: Lasso 1581, fol. 10r.

CONCORDANCE: Lasso 1582, fol. 11r.

MODEL: RISM 1565[11], p. 25 (anon.; see no. [27] in this edition).

NOTES ON THE TEXT: For the annotated text and translation, see no. [27]. Lasso 1581 and Lasso 1582 have one strophe; the anonymous model has four strophes.
    1. "stralucenti" is "tralucente" in RISM 1565[11].
    2. "Tienemi mente" is "Tienemi a mente" in RISM 1565[11].
    3. "Guardam'un poc'a me, fami contiento" is "Guardam'un poco a me, fame contento" in RISM 1565[11].

NOTES ON THE MUSIC: M. 5, Canto, cautionary flat before note 1 in Lasso 1581 and Lasso 1582.   M. 22, Canto, note 1, two crome in Lasso 1581 and Lasso 1582, notes 2–3, semiminim in Lasso 1581 and Lasso 1582—corrected according to m. 31, which matches the rhythmic declamation in the model (no. [27], m. 18).

[17] *Ogni giorno m'han ditt'a chi favelli*

Ogni giorno m'han ditt'a chi favelli,
Dici che m'ami e voi ch'io stia con teco.

"Io lo voria veder," disse lo cieco,
Che questo dir è poi tenerm'a[1] bada.
Dic'el spagnolo, "mi par esser nada."

SOURCE: Lasso 1581, fols. 6v–7r.

CONCORDANCE: Lasso 1582, fol. 7v.

NOTES ON THE TEXT: Lasso 1581 and Lasso 1582 have one strophe.   Mm. 21–23, Tenore, second repeat symbol for the phrase "che questo dir," Lasso 1582.

1. "tenerm'a" is "tenervi' a" in Canto, Lasso 1581 and Lasso 1582.

The complete poem of four strophes is located in Cimello 1545, p. 2:

1. Ogni iuorno[a] m'an ditto a chi favelli
   Dici cha m'ami e vuoi ch'io stia con teco.

   "Io lo vorria veder," disse lo ceco,
   Che questo dire è poi tenermi a bada.
   Dice 'l spagnolo, "mi pareze nada."[b]

2. Poi vengo dove stai senza civelli,[c]
   E mai me guardi, e saccio che t'arreco.
   "Io lo vorria veder," . . .

3. Se non mostri l'amore con cobelli,[d]
   'No gotto 'nanzi[e] vozera[f] de greco.[g]

   "Io lo vorria veder," . . .

4. Una de due, o mi lo mostra cetto,[h]
   O state cha[i] mesto me chiù[j] l'aspetto.

   "Io lo vorria veder," . . .

1. Every day the ones you talk to have told me
   You say you love me and want me to stay with you.

   "I would like to see that," said the blind man,
   For to say this is to keep me waiting.
   As the Spaniard says, "I think it's nothing."

2. When I come without procurers to where you stay,
   You never look at me, but I know I provoke you.
   "I would like to see that," . . .

3. If you don't show love for trinkets,
   Then I'll ply you with Greek wine—first a goblet, then a flask.
   "I would like to see that," . . .

4. Make up your mind, either show it to me right away,
   Or rest assured that I'll stir up trouble the more I wait for it.
   "I would like to see that," . . .

_____

[a]*iuorno,* Neapolitan for *giorno.*

[b]*mi pareze nada,* Spanish for *mi par esser niente.* This line alludes to the saying "Dir come lo Spagnuolo," which means to undervalue everything (Torr.P, 2:198).

[c]*civelli,* from *accivire.*

[d]*cobelli* (alt. sp. of *covelle*).

[e] *'nanzi,* Neapolitan for *innanzi.*

[f]*vozera,* from *borraccia.*

[g]*greco*—Greek wine, according to the following proverb, was prized in Italy: "Sopra ogni vino, il greco è divino" (Sper.P, 225).

[h]*cetto,* old form of *presto.*

[i]*cha,* Neapolitan for *ché.*

[j]*chiù,* Neapolitan for *più.*

NOTES ON THE MUSIC: No errors.

[18] *Par ch'hai lasciato de non t'affacciare*

1. Par ch'hai lasciato de non t'affacciare,[1]

   Per far sapere ca si'[2] malatesta.[3]
   Deh, poverella con tanto susiego,[4]
   Non far che con te sape[5] lo Don Diego.[6]

2. Forse te credi di me laniare,[7]
   Che me stà inchiusa[8] come stess'in[9] cella.
   Deh, poverella . . .

3. Tira, cà te dovrissi vergognare,
   Tutto lo giorno farsi Iacovella.[10]
   Deh, poverella . . .

1. It seems you've decided not to peek out the window,
   To let it be known that you're perverse.
   Ah, poor girl with such haughty airs,
   Don't do it, because someone knows Don Diego is with you.

2. Perhaps you think of torturing me,
   Cloistered like this in the cellar.
   Ah, poor girl . . .

3. Go away, for you should be ashamed of yourself,
   Weaving clever intrigues all day long.
   Ah, poor girl . . .

4. Donna[11] che face quello che non suole,
   Ò t'hà gabbato, ò gabbare ti vuole.[12]

   E senti due parolle[13] se tu voi,
   Cà[14] saccio quante[15] para[16] fan tre boi.[17]

4. A woman who does more than usual
   Has either deceived you or intends to deceive
   you.
   Redouble the stakes if you like,
   Because I know how many pairs three oxen
   make.

SOURCE: Lasso 1581, fols. 4v–5r.

CONCORDANCE: Lasso 1582, fols. 4v–5r.

NOTES ON THE TEXT: Accents on "stà," "hà," "ò," and "cà" are in Lasso 1581 and Lasso 1582.

1. *affacciare*, Neapolitan for *far capolino*, literally playing peekaboo or, as in this case, flirting from the window, a habit of courtesans. Instead of enticing men from her usual place, the courtesan in this poem has retreated to a hideaway and has taken a Spanish lover, Don Diego. The jealous client who narrates the poem knows what she is up to because of her change in behavior.

2. *si'*, Neapolitan for *sia*.

3. *malatesta*—"To be wicked and obstinate in any purpose whatsoever; gingling [jingling] with Malatesta, unlucky head, the name of an honourable family, and mala, the adjective, wicked and perverse by way of drollery" (Torr.P, 2:22).

4. *susiego*, derived from the Spanish *sosiego*.

5. *sape*, Neapolitan for *sa* (from *sapere*).

6. During the sixteenth century, after the Spaniard had become a stock character in Italian comedy, the metaphorical phrase "fare il Don Diego" was used to refer to someone who makes amorous advances with exaggerated ceremony in the Spanish manner, that is, bowing and hand-kissing (Cro.S, 178).

7. *laniare*, literally to tear to pieces, figuratively to torment cruelly.

8. "stà inchiusa" is "st'inchiusa" in Tenore and Basso, Lasso 1581 and Lasso 1582. In Neapolitan dialect *'nchiuso* has the figurative meaning *chiuso in convento* (Alta.D, 154), which creates an ironic and irreverent paradox in this strophe. The real trysting place would be a hideaway like the cellar, as *cella* has been translated; but *cella* is also used here allusively to mean convent cell, which reinforces the paradox. Yet another meaning of *cella* is beehive, which sweetens the image of a hidden love nest.

9. *stess'in—stesso* is an old Neapolitan form of *questo*.

10. *farsi Iacovella*, literally to become Jacovella, a sly, cunning character type in Neapolitan comedy, given to intrigue and trickery (Mal.P, 1:655).

11. *donna*—Another meaning of *donna* is the queen of cards, who, like the courtesan, is fickle and capricious.

12. The entire couplet is a variant of a popular saying of the time. Basile has the ogress quote it in the tale *Le tre corone*, after she discovers her house has been tidied up: "Chi te fa chello che fare non sole, ò t'ha gabbato, ò gabbare te vole!" (Bas.C, 326–27).

13. *parolle* (alt. sp. of *parole*), doubled stake in dice games played in sixteenth-century Naples (Bas.C, 735). In some Italian gambling games, *parole* can mean a redoubled stake (Batt.G).

14. *Cà*, Neapolitan for *perchè*.

15. "quante" is "quanto" in m. 88, all parts, Lasso 1581, and in Canto, Alto, and Tenore, Lasso 1582 (cf. m. 93, where text reads "quante" in all parts).

16. *para*, Neapolitan for *paio*.

17. *boi* (alt. sp. of *voje*), Neapolitan for *bue*. The entire line is a popular saying that means, "I know what you are up to," or "to know as much as another, to see as far in a millstone as another" (Torr.P, 2:22).

NOTES ON THE MUSIC: Mensuration sign is ¢ in Canto, Lasso 1582.   M. 34, Alto, double bar with no repeat sign in Lasso 1581 and Lasso 1582.   M. 77, Tenore, double bar with repeat sign in Lasso 1581 and Lasso 1582.   M. 85, Canto and Tenore, double bar after note 2 in Lasso 1581 and Lasso 1582.

[19] *Saccio 'na cosa ch'è di legn'e tonda*

Saccio 'na[1] cosa ch'è di legn'e tonda,
E con ferretto volt'a funicella.

   Nenina,[2] o pazzarella,
   Ch'è strombolo[3] che volt'o argatella.

SOURCE: Lasso 1581, fol. 4r.

CONCORDANCE: Lasso 1582, fol. 4r.

MODEL: Fontana 1545, no. 14 (see no. [28] in this edition).

NOTES ON THE TEXT: For the annotated text and translation, see no. [28]. Lasso 1581 and Lasso 1582 have one strophe; the model by Fontana has four.   Mm. 4–5 and 11–12, Canto, Alto, and Tenore, repeat symbol is used for the phrase "saccio 'na cosa," Lasso 1582.   Mm. 22–24, Canto and Tenore, repeat symbol is used for the phrase "Nenin'o pazzarella," Lasso 1582.

    1. " 'na" is "una" in Canto, Lasso 1581; 'na is Neapolitan for una.

    2. "Nenina" is " 'Nevina," Fontana 1545.

    3. "strombolo" is given in abbreviated form, Lasso 1581 and Lasso 1582; resolved to "stronbolo" in final phrase of Alto, Lasso 1582, and once to "strombolo" in Basso, Lasso 1581 and Lasso 1582.

NOTES ON THE MUSIC: No errors.

[20] S'io fusse ciaul'et tu lo campanile

S'io fusse ciaul'[1] et tu lo campanile,	If I were a magpie and you the bell tower,
Ben spesso, spesso te voria montare.[2]	Full many a time I would like to rise up you.
Tutto lo giorno ben vorria cantare,	*All day long I would like to sing*
Et sempre mai saltare,	*And continually to leap,*
Et spesso te basciare,	*To kiss you again and again,*
Et poi la sera nel pertus'[3] entrare.	*Then at night to slip into the chamber.*

SOURCE: Lasso 1581, fol. 7r.

CONCORDANCE: Lasso 1582, fol. 8r.

NOTES ON THE TEXT: Lasso 1581 and Lasso 1582 have one strophe.   Mm. 39–43, Canto, repeat symbol for the phrase "et poi la sera nel pertus' entrare," Lasso 1582.

    1. *ciaul'* (alt. sp. of *ciaola*), means *gazza* in sixteenth-century Neapolitan dialect and later *corvo* or *cornacchia* (Penz.P, 2:64). The phallic motif of wishful transformation into a bird to gain entry (in the cage, nest, or window) is common in Italian lyric poems, both literary and popular. Diverse birds populate these poems, ranging from the lecherous swallow to the crafty crow and the chattering magpie. For a discussion of the interrelationships between Neapolitan poems with this motif, see Elena Ferrari Barassi, "La villanella napoletana nella testimonianza di un letterato," *Nuova rivista musicale italiana* 6 (1968): 1083–86. Various Italian and Neapolitan idioms use the metaphor of the crow or the magpie in the bell tower, for example, "esser cornacchia da campanile" (to be a crafty person) and "fare comm'a ciaola 'n campanaro" (to pretend to be deaf or to be firm in purpose). The "magpie" in this poem has all these qualities as evidenced in his chattering refrain, which reveals a cunning plan of seduction. For a *villanesca* in which the protagonist is an astute female magpie, see Nola's *Madonna mia ciaula de campanaro* (NolaO, vol. 1, no. 21).

    2. *montare* can mean to copulate.

    3. *pertus'* (=*pertuso*), Neapolitan dialect for *pertugio* or *piccolo vano*. In this case it is literally the hollow bell chamber but with euphemistic overtones. Pertuso was a place in Naples near the Montesanto Church and derived its name from a gap in the gate that served as a popular meeting place for challenges and duels (Penz.P, 1:67). Malpertugio is the name of the whore's alley in Boccaccio's *Decameron*, second day, fifth story.

NOTES ON THE MUSIC: No errors in Lasso 1581 and 1582. The repeat of the final strain, mm. 44–51, is written out in all parts except Canto, Lasso 1581 and 1582.

[21] S'io ti vedess'una sol volt'il giorno

S'io ti vedess'una sol volt'il giorno,	If I could see you only once a day,
Contento ne staria[1] tutta la sera.	I would remain satisfied all evening long.
Fa ru re ra, fa ru re ra,	*Fa ru re ra, fa ru re ra,*
Bella fior di primavera.	*Fair springtime blossom.*

SOURCE: Lasso 1581, fol. 9v.

Notes on the Text: Lasso 1581 and Lasso 1582 have one strophe.
    1. *staria*, first person, present conditional of *stare* in Neapolitan.

Notes on the Music: No errors in Lasso 1581 and Lasso 1582. Another setting of the same strophe may be found in Nola 1545(2), no. 21, but it was not Lasso's model (see NolaO, vol. 1, no. 42).

[22] *S'io ve dico ca sete la chiù bella*

S'io ve dico ca sete la chiù[1] bella	If I tell you that you are the fairest
Di tutte belle al mondo mai son nate,	Of all beauties ever born in the world,
Dico lo ver'e voi ve ne sdegnate.	*I tell the truth and you get angry.*

Source: Lasso 1581, fol. 2r.

Concordance: Lasso 1582, fol. 2r.

Notes on the Text: Lasso 1581 and Lasso 1582 have one strophe.   Mm. 23–24, Tenore, repeat symbol is used for the phrase "dico lo ver'e voi," Lasso 1582.
    1. *ca sete la chiù*, Neapolitan for *che siete la più.*

Notes on the Music: No errors in Lasso 1581 and Lasso 1582.

[23] *Tutto lo dì mi dici, "canta, canta"*

Tutto lo dì mi dici, "canta, canta."	All day long you tell me, "Sing, sing."
Non vedi ca non posso refiatare?	Don't you see that I'm all out of breath?
A che tanto cantare?	*What's the use of so much singing?*
Voria che mi dicessi, "sona, sona,"	*I wish you would tell me, "Play, play"—*
Non le campan'a nona,[1]	*Not the bells at none,*
Ma so[2] *cimbalo*[3] *tuo.*	*But on your cembalo.*
O! se campo ri ro ro ri[4] *rogne,*[5]	*Ah! if I survive the scra-, scra-, scratching,*
S'io t'haggio sott'a 'st'ogne.[6]	*Let me but hold you in my clutches.*

Source: Lasso 1581, fol. 3v.

Concordance: Lasso 1582, fol. 3v.

Notes on the Text: Lasso 1581 and Lasso 1582 have one strophe.   Mm. 7–8, Canto, Tenore, and Basso, repeat symbol is used for the phrase "non vedi ca non posso," Lasso 1582.   Mm. 21 and 25, Tenore, "Non" included under repeat symbol, Lasso 1582.
    1. *nona*—None is the ninth hour of the daily Office celebrated in monasteries at 3 p.m.
    2. *so*, alt. sp. of *su.*
    3. *cimbalo*—This word in the singular has two literal meanings, cymbal or cembalo (harpsichord), either of which would be viable in the context of the poem. Cembalo is the preferred translation, especially when understood in connection with the Neapolitan idiom "sonare de zimbaro (cembalo)," which means figuratively to be light-fingered (Bas.C, 769). Allusion to nimble touching of the instrument (i.e., the woman's body) in this line effectively anticipates the carnal images of scratching and clawing in the final couplet. Cf. the personification of cembalo in the Tuscan idiom "non sono mica un cembalo" (I'm not just something to be played with). The alternative, cymbal, would make patent the lover's preference for an arousing sonority traditionally associated with Bacchus and fabled to incite orgiastic behavior; moreover, it would preserve the salient point of comparison with the calming tones of monastery bells. Also, *cimbalo* pronounced with a Neapolitan accent sounds like *zimbello*, an alluring decoy to attract birds.
    4. *ri ro ro ri*, onomatopoetic syllables to suggest the sound of scratching.
    5. *rogne*—The itch of carnal desire that the following Neapolitan proverbs claim knows no rest: "E come rogna, che, quanto gratti più, più da prurito" and "O rogna, che se sbatte, che t'abbruscia cchiù assai, quanto cchiù gratte," which mean the more you scratch, the more it itches (Sper.P, 217).
    6. *'st'ogne*, Neapolitan for *quest'unghie.*

Notes on the Music: No errors in Lasso 1581 and Lasso 1582.
    Lasso's setting of the same poem for eight voices is a reworking of his four-part setting. It was included in a group of *canzone a otto* at the end of *Libro de villanelle* (see LassoW, 10:130).

Neapolitan Models for Lasso's *Villanelle*

[24] *Ad altre lo voi dare 'ste passate (Nola)*

1. Ad altre lo voi dare 'ste passate,
   Che non con no[1] che voglio lo cocucco.[2]
       La trich'e trach'e[3] trucco,
       Ch'altro sta dentro et io da fore allucco.[4]

2. Tu te credevi aver me ce incapato,[5]
   Va', figlia mia, cha[6] te do truc mucco.[7]
       La trich'e . . .

3. A vive melle[8] tese le biscate,[9]
   Come se fosse qualche mammalucche.[10]
       La trich'e . . .

4. Femina bella, civala[11] et cucuvaya,[12]
   Ad ogne tempo te danno la baya.[13]
       La trich'e . . .

1. To everyone you give the same treatment,
   But I certainly don't want the humbug.
       Tricky-tracky trickery,
       The other one is in and I'm out, yelling.

2. You think you've lassoed me;
   Go, my girl, or else I'll send you flying.
       Tricky . . .

3. With fresh honey you laid sticky traps,
   As if I were some simpleton.
       Tricky . . .

4. Winsome wench, lazy slut, whore—
   At any time they'll play a trick on you.
       Tricky . . .

SOURCE: Nola 1545(2), no. 12 (unicum).

NOTES ON THE TEXT: The refrain cue is given as "ch'altro" in strophes 2–4.

1. "Che non con no" is "che non con non no" in mm. 11–12.

2. *cocucco*, from *cuccare*.

3. *trich'e trach'e* (alt. sp. of *tricche tracche*), onomatopoetic syllables that imitate the clicking sound made by the pieces used in playing trictrac, an old variety of backgammon. In this poem the sounds of the syllables suggest that business with courtesans is tricky, like gambling. These syllables were also used to denote firecrackers, e.g., *saltarelli* (jumping jacks), or to imitate their sound (Bas.C, 431 and 763). *La trichetraccara* is a woman who sells firecrackers (Mal.P, 679).

4. *allucco*, Neapolitan for *gridare*.

5. *incapato*, Neapolitan, from *incappiare*.

6. *cha*, Neapolitan for *perchè*.

7. *truc mucco*, Neapolitan expression for a "stroke in billiards when one's own ball remains in the place from which one drives away that of the opponent" (Penz.P, 1:187 n. 4). In this poem it is used as a slang metaphorical expression for being hurried off in a different direction (cf. Penz.P, 2:6). *Trucco-mucco* also means dirty trick (Bas.C, 763).

8. *melle*, alt. sp. of *miele*.

9. *biscate* (alt. sp. of *viscate*), Neapolitan for *vischio*. *Cosa da bisca* is a metaphorical expression for a carnal act (Mal.P, 681).

10. *mammalucche*—Mamelukes were slave warriors from Caucasia who usurped the throne of Egypt in 1254. The word taken in its historical sense connotes savage ferocity, since Mamelukes carried long sabers with double-edged cutting points. In colloquial Italian *mammalucco*, for its sound, had come to mean simpleton by this time (Penz.P, 2:134).

11. *civala*, alt. sp. of *ciabatta*.

12. *cucuvaya* (alt. sp. of *coccovaya*), Neapolitan for *civetta*, which is literally flirt and metaphorically whore (Bas.C, 706).

13. *baya* (alt. sp. of *baia*)—*dar la baia* means "to break a jest on one" (Torr.P, 2:9).

NOTES ON THE MUSIC: No errors.

[25] *Ecco la nimph'Ebraica chiamata (Nola)*

1. Ecco la nimph'Ebraica[1] chiamata,
   Più brutt'assai de Menech'e de Chiara.[2]
       Lingnite,[3] pingnite,[4] stringnite,[5]
       Olà, mendrangola[6] scioffata,[7]
       Che tenne vidi ca si' 'namorata.[8]

1. Here is the nymph called Ebraica,
   Much more ugly than Meneca and Chiara.
       Titillate, instigate, strangulate,
       Hey there, crippled mandrake,
       How could you think of falling in love?

2. Dellegia[9] sempre et sempre è dellegiata,
   Sta zandragliosa,[10] faccie da ianara.

   Lingnite . . .

3. Occhi de bove, naserchia[11] accorciata,
   Boccha de sbecchia,[12] barba de cochiara.[13]

   Lingnite . . .

4. Sia benedicto chi te fece stare,
   Quatro mis'a la cener'accovare.[14]

   Lingnite . . .

2. Forever mocking and always mocked
   Is this ragamuffin, her face fit for a witch.

   Titillate . . .

3. Big cow eyes, flat pug nose,
   Withered mouth, protruding chin.

   Titillate . . .

4. Blessed be the one who made you stay
   For four months squatting idly by the fire.

   Titillate . . .

SOURCE: Nola 1545(1), no. 17 (unicum).

NOTES ON THE TEXT:

1. *nimph'Ebraica* (alt. sp. of *ninfa Ebraica*), literally a young and slender Hebrew girl but figuratively a "water nymph" of easy virtue who worked the hot baths in Naples. Del Tufo, when praising Neapolitan bath attendants in his *Ritratto* (1588), referred to female bathers as nymphs: "So other nymphs often go and take the baths in these hot and perfumed waters, and in these elegant baths are beds made ready by these same attendants" (quoted in Penz.P, 1:303). The moralist Tomaso Garzoni, when complaining about the baths in *Piazza universale* (1589), leveled his accusations at "pimps who keep rooms for hire, uniting external cleanliness with internal uncleanliness in those baths which are dens of all shameful and dishonest lusts" (quoted in Penz.P, 1:303). The nymph in this poem has a face and body ravaged by sexually transmitted diseases, rampant in Naples, which make her appear old and worn before her time.

2. The names of the women are not capitalized in Nola 1545(1); they were probably local persons of some notoriety. Meneca is a Neapolitan nickname for Domenica.

3. *lingnite*, from *lignere* (*lusingare*).

4. *pingnite*, from *spingere*.

5. *stringnite*, from *stringere*.

6. *mendrangola* (alt. sp. of *mandrangola* or *mandragora*), a narcotic medicinal herb, often with a forked root, and fabled to utter a deadly shriek when plucked from the ground. In this poem mandrake is an abusive word for an odious person.

7. *scioffata*, Neapolitan for *sciancato*.

8. *si' 'namorata*, Neapolitan for *sia innamorata*.

9. *dellegia*, from *dileggiare*.

10. *zandragliosa* (alt. sp. of *zantragliosa*), Neapolitan for *stracciona*.

11. *naserchia* (alt. sp. of *nasorchia*), Neapolitan for *naso schiacciato*.

12. *sbecchia*, Neapolitan for *invecchiare*.

13. *cochiara* (alt. sp. of *cucchiaio*)—*barba di cocchiara* was a colloquial expression in sixteenth-century Naples. See, for example, act 2, scene 5, of *Il candelaio* (1582), a Neapolitan comedy by Giordano Bruno.

14. *accovare*, Neapolitan for *accucciare*. *Covacenere* is a person who sits by the fire instead of working.

NOTES ON THE MUSIC: No errors.

[26] *O belle, fusa! chi ne vo' accatare?* (Nola)

1. O belle, fusa! chi ne vo'[1] accatare?[2]
   Noi le vendimo queste fusa in prova.

   Son fusa nova,
   Voi le provare?
   Venitell'a pigliare,[3]
   Le dam'in prova.

2. Piglialo tu e ve'[4] se 'l poi piegare,
   Et tre le damo a grano[5] com'a l'ova.[6]

   Son fusa nova . . .

3. Se tu le provi donna a comparare,
   Questo è legname che non se ne trova.

   Son fusa nova . . .

1. O beauties, spindles! Who wants to buy some?
   We are selling these spindles on approval.

   They are new spindles;
   Do you want to test them?
   Come take them;
   We offer them on approval.

2. Take one and see if you can bend it,
   We give three of them for coppers or eggs.

   They are new spindles . . .

3. Lady, if you put them to the test,
   This is woodwork beyond compare.

   They are new spindles . . .

4. Cha[7] sono fusa d'un certo paese,
Che quanto più de file più stan tese.[8]
 	
   Son fusa nova . . .
	4. Here are spindles from a certain town;
	The more you spin them, the more they stay taut.
	
	   They are new spindles . . .

SOURCE: Nola 1545(1), no. 13 (unicum).

NOTES ON THE TEXT: Mm. 23 (note 3)–28, Bassus, printer's erroneous text underlay is "Son fusa nova, voi le provare, venitell'a pigliare." In imitative textures like this one, Nola normally synchronized text declamation in the two parts, which are homorhythmic.

    1. *vo'*, Neapolitan for *vuole;* apostrophe supplied.

    2. *accatare* (alt. sp. of *accattare*), Neapolitan for *comprare*.

    3. "pigliare" is "pilgliare" in all parts.

    4. *ve'*, Neapolitan for *vedi;* apostrophe supplied.

    5. *grano*, a Neapolitan coin made of copper in use from the fourteenth to the nineteenth century and worth one-tenth of a *carlino*, that is, a trifle (Mal.P, 1:668).

    6. *ova*—During Carnival in Naples it was the custom for courtesans, to whom this song is addressed, to fling eggs of sweet water from their windows to the passersby (Penz.P, 1:164).

    7. *cha*, old form of *qua*.

    8. Spindle proverbs commonly rely on phallic metaphors, for example, "far le fusa storte," which means to be unfaithful or literally to make crooked spindles (Torr.P, 2:68).

NOTES ON THE MUSIC: M. 6, Cantus, note 3, no accidental.

[27] *O occhi manza mia, cigli dorati (Anon.)*

1. O occhi manza[1] mia,[2] cigli dorati,
  O faccia d'una luna[3] tralucente,[4]
 	
    Tienimi a mente,[5]
    Gioia mia bella,
    Guardam'un poco a me, fame contento.[6]
	1. O my beloved's eyes, set in gilded lashes,
	  O face luminous as the moon,
	
	    Remember me,
	    My lovely treasure,
	    Look after me for a little while, satisfy me.

2. O bocca come zuccaro impanato,
  O canna[7] che specchiare[8] fai la gente,
 	
    Tienimi . . .
	2. O mouth like sugarloaf,
	  O throat that you draw crowds to suck,
	
	    Remember me . . .

3. O pietto che conforti gli amalati,[9]
  Pieno di fiori et dolci acque sorgenti,
 	
    Tienimi . . .
	3. O bosom that consoles the suffering,
	  Full of blossoms and fresh spring waters,
	
	    Remember me . . .

4. Per tante quante gratie che tu hai,
  Ricordati di me, perchè tu sai
 	
    Che son galante.
    Gioia mia bella,
    Guardam'un poco a me, fame contento.
	4. For the infinite graces that you possess,
	  Remember me, because you know
	
	    That I am gallant.
	    My lovely treasure,
	    Look after me for a little while, satisfy me.

SOURCE: RISM 1565[11], p. 25.

CONCORDANCES: RISM 1557[20] (C), p. 32; RISM 1560[13] (T), p. 5; RISM 1562[12], p. 5; RISM 1566[6], p. 5; RISM 1571[6], p. 5.

NOTES ON THE TEXT: Text underlay is misaligned throughout the refrain in RISM 1557[20]. For a facsimile reproduction of the Cantus, the only extant partbook of RISM 1557[20], see Card.CV, vol. 2, pl. 17.

    1. *manza*, another form of *amanza* (*donna amata*) but punning on *manza*, which means heifer.

    2. Repeat symbol is used for the phrase "O occhi manza mia" in RISM 1557[20].

    3. Repeat symbol is used for the phrase "O faccia d'una luna" in RISM 1557[20].

    4. "tralucente" is "stralucenti" in Lasso's text (see no. [16]).

    5. "tienimi a mente" is "tienimi" in Canto (first strophe only), RISM 1560[13], RISM 1566[6], and RISM 1571[6]; "tienemi mente" in Lasso's text (see no. [16]). Neapolitan for *ricordare* (Mal.P, 1:658).

    6. The phrase is "Guardam'un poc'a me, fami contiento" in Lasso's text (see no. [16]).

    7. *canna*, Neapolitan for *gola*.

    8. *specchiare*, Neapolitan for *apecchiare*, literally to suck like a bee.

9. ''amalati'' is ''amalti'' in all parts, RISM 1571[6].

Another reading of "O occhi manza mia" is located in a miscellany of popular poetry: *Lamento che fece li mercanti al Mercato di Rovere . . . con alquante canzoni napolitane bellissime* (Venice: [Domenico de Franceschi,] 1585), fol. 4r (exemplar in Rome, Biblioteca Universitaria Alessandrina, Misc. Cerrotti, XIII.a.58/40). The dialectal elements of the poem are preserved in this reading. Strophe 3, line 2, and strophe 4, line 3, differ from their counterparts in extant musical settings:

1. O occhi manza mia ciglia adorate,
   O faccia come Luna risplendente,
     Tienemi a mente gioia mia bella,
     Guardami un poco a me, e me fammi contiento.

2. O bocca come un zuccaro impaniato,
   O chana che specchiar tu fai la gente,
     Tienemi . . .

3. O petto che conforti gli ammalati,
   Pieno di fiorite frondi a chesta gente.
     Tienemi . . .

4. Per tante quante gratie che tu hai,
   Ricordati di me, perché tu sai
     Io son amante fido, e costante,
     Guardami un poco a me, e me fammi contiento.

NOTES ON THE MUSIC: Mm. 19 and 25, Basso, notes 3 and 5, no accidental.

[28] *Sacio 'na cosa ch'è di legno e tonda (Fontana)*

1. Sacio 'na[1] cosa ch'è di legno e tonda,
   E con fereto, volt'a fonicella.[2]
     'Nevina,[3] o pazarella,
     Ch'è strombolo[4] che volta, o argatella.[5]

2. Sacio 'na cosa e se usa in tutto il mondo,
   E dentro ce se pon la cuzinella.[6]
     'Nevina, o pazarella,
     Fosse un pignato[7] questa, o 'na scutella.[8]

3. De pane e caso[9] fusse pepe[10] fondo,
   Con fecato e sofrirss'anatrella.[11]
     'Nevina, o pazarella,
     È gratinata questa o tomazella.[12]

4. De presuto[13] de porco ben tridatta,
   Se fa 'na cosa con pepe e salata,
     Intro un stentin[14] serata.
     'Nevina, ch'è saucizia sopresata![15]

1. I know something that's wooden and round
   With a curved tip, whirled by a thin string.
     Guess, you little fool,
     It's a spinning top, O clever girl.

2. I know something used the whole world over,
   In it one puts a little ham shank.
     Guess, you little fool,
     This would be a soup pot or a soup bowl.

3. Of bread and cheese, it would be deeply spiced,
   Mixed with liver and sauteed duckling.
     Guess, you little fool,
     This is an au gratin dish or tomasella.

4. Of a ham joint ground up well,
   Something is made with pepper and salt,
     In an intestine tightly fit.
     Guess what, it's a pork sausage!

SOURCE: Fontana 1545, no. 14 (unicum).

NOTES ON THE TEXT:
   1. *'na*, Neapolitan for *una*.
   2. *fonicella*, Neapolitan for *funicella*.
   3. *'Nevina* (alt. sp. of *'nnevena*), Neapolitan for *indovinare*; "'Nevina" is "Nenina" in Lasso's text (see no. [19]).
   4. *strombolo*, Neapolitan for *trottolina*.
   5. ''argatella'' is ''Argatella'' in all parts.
   6. *cuzinella*, Neapolitan diminutive of *coscia*.
   7. *pignato*, a wooden pot. Ham was used for flavoring in a Neapolitan cabbage soup called *pignata grassa*.
   8. *scutella*, alt. sp. of *scodella*.
   9. *caso*, Neapolitan for *cacio*.
   10. ''pepe'' is ''Pepe'' in all parts.
   11. ''anatrella'' is ''Anatrella'' in all parts.
   12. *tomazella* (alt. sp. of *tomasella* or *tomacella*), a popular casserole of the time often made of minced pork liver and cheese, seasoned with ginger, saffron, and pepper (Pra.V, 988).
   13. *presuto*, Neapolitan for *prosciutto*.
   14. *stentin*, Neapolitan for *intestine*.
   15. *saucizia sopresata*, Neapolitan for *salsiccia soprassata*, sausage made from a pig's head in the region of Nola. In this poem it is a phallic metaphor.

NOTES ON THE MUSIC: No errors. For a facsimile reproduction of the Tenor, see Card.CV, vol. 2, pl. 26.

Intabulations for Lute

[29] *La cortesia*

SOURCE: Phal & Bell 1571₆, fol. 52v.

ATTRIBUTION: Orlando.

INTABULATOR: Sixt Kargel.

VOCAL MODEL: see no. [1].

CRITICAL NOTES: M. 5, chord 2, note 4, *a* on g' string—*d* supplied by analogy with m. 13. M. 21, first rhythm symbol is a semiminim, second rhythm symbol is a croma. M. 29, chord 4, note 3, *c* on d' string—*b* supplied by analogy with m. 34.

[30] *Madonna mia pietà*

SOURCE: Kargel 1574₁, fol. D4, no. 20.

ATTRIBUTION: none.

INTABULATOR: Sixt Kargel.

VOCAL MODEL: see no. [2].

CRITICAL NOTES: M. 26, chord 1, note 3, *2* on d' string—*1* supplied by analogy with m. 33.

[31] *Madonna mia pietà*

SOURCE: Adriansen 1584₆, fol. 48v.

ATTRIBUTION: Orlando di Lasso (in table of contents).

INTABULATOR: Emanuel Adriansen.

VOCAL MODEL: see no. [2].

CRITICAL NOTES: (Canto) M. 9, chord 2, note 3, *c* on e' string—*b* supplied by analogy with m. 4. M. 19, first rhythm symbol lacks dot. M. 28, beat 1 has *a* on g string, no rest; chord 1, note 1, *a* lacking on d string—supplied from vocal model. M. 29, chord 2, rhythm symbol lacks dot.

(Alto) M. 13, chord 3, note 3, *b* on d' string. M. 15, beat 2, note 4, *b* on d' string. Mm. 25 and 32, chord 3, note 2, *a* on a string. M. 33, chord 5, note 2, *c* lacking on f string—supplied by analogy with m. 26.

(Basso) Mm. 4 and 9, chord 2, note 2, *c* on e string. M. 18, chord 3, note 3, *c* on e string. M. 25, chord 4, note 1, *a* on G string, note 3, *d* on e string. M. 32, chord 4, note 1, *a* on G string.

[32] *Madonna mia pietà*

SOURCE: Adriansen 1584₆, fol. 13v.

ATTRIBUTION: Orlando di Lasso (in table of contents).

INTABULATOR: Emanuel Adriansen.

VOCAL MODEL: see no. [2].

CRITICAL NOTES: (Lute) M. 20, chord 1, note 2, *i* on a string—*a* supplied from vocal model. M. 30, chord 3, note 2, *a* lacking on a string—supplied by analogy with m. 23. M. 32, chord 1, note 2, *f* lacking on f string—supplied by analogy with m. 25.

[33] *Sto core mio*

SOURCE: Phal & Bell 1571₆, fol. 52v.

ATTRIBUTION: Orlando.

INTABULATOR: Sixt Kargel.

VOCAL MODEL: see no. [4].

CRITICAL NOTES: M. 17, chord 3, note 2, *d* on a string—*c* supplied by analogy with m. 22. M. 21, beat 1, letters for all notes placed one string higher, except chord 1, note 2, which is *d* on a string.

[34] *Tu sai madona*

SOURCE: Phal & Bell 1571₆, fol. 52r.

ATTRIBUTION: Orlando.

INTABULATOR: Sixt Kargel.

VOCAL MODEL: see no. [5].

CRITICAL NOTES: M. 26, rhythm symbol is dotted minim. M. 30, chord 1, note 4, *d* on g' string—*a* supplied from vocal model. M. 31, chord 3, note 4, *a* lacking on g' string—supplied from vocal model. M. 37, chord 1, note 4, *e* on d' string—*d* supplied by analogy with m. 45. M. 43, chord 2, note 2, *d* lacking on a string—supplied by analogy with m. 35.

[35] *Tu traditore*

SOURCE: Phal & Bell 1571₆, fol. 53r.

ATTRIBUTION: Orlando.

INTABULATOR: Sixt Kargel.

VOCAL MODEL: see no. [6].

CRITICAL NOTES: Mm. 10 and 16, chord 2, note 2, *f* on a string—*d* supplied from vocal model. M. 20, beat 1, note 2, *c* on g' string—*d* supplied by analogy with m. 14.

Intabulations for Four-Course Cittern

[36] *La cortesia*

SOURCE: Phal & Bell 1570₃, fol. 84r.

ATTRIBUTION: none.

INTABULATOR: anon.

VOCAL MODEL: see no. [1].

CRITICAL NOTES: M. 19, chord 3, note 2, *d* on g string. Mm. 29 and 34, chord 1, *a* on b string.

[37] *Madona mia pietà*

SOURCE: Phal & Bell 1570₃, fol. 82v.

ATTRIBUTION: none.

INTABULATOR: anon.

VOCAL MODEL: see no. [2].

CRITICAL NOTES: Mm. 1 and 6, chord 5, note 2, *d* on g string. Mm. 23 and 30, chord 4, *c* on b string.

[38] *Madonna mia pietà*

SOURCE: Kargel 1578₄, no. 32.

CONCORDANCE: Kargel 1580₂, no. 32.

ATTRIBUTION: none.

INTABULATOR: Sixt Kargel.

VOCAL MODEL: see no. [2].

CRITICAL NOTES: M. 4, chord 4, note 4, *1* on a string—*3* supplied by analogy with m. 9 and 1580 reprint. M. 6, chord 4, rhythm symbol is minim. M. 9, chord 2, lacks semiminim rhythm symbol.

[39] *Sto core mio*

SOURCE: Phal & Bell 1582₅, fol. 28r.

ATTRIBUTION: none.

INTABULATOR: anon.

VOCAL MODEL: see no. [4].

CRITICAL NOTES: M. 11, chord consisting of *g* on e′ string, *e* on d′ string, *a* on g string, and *e* on a string beneath rhythm symbol, no rest. Mm. 12 (beat 2)–14 (chord 1), rhythmic symbols are displaced back by one note.

[40] *Tu traditora*

SOURCE: Phal & Bell 1570₃, fol. 83r.

ATTRIBUTION: none.

INTABULATOR: anon.

VOCAL MODEL: see no. [6].

CRITICAL NOTES: M. 11, beat 2, rhythm symbol is semiminim. M. 21, beat 2, rhythm symbol is croma.

Intabulations for Six-Course Cittern

[41] *La cortesia*

SOURCE: Kargel & Lais 1575₃, fol. D3v, no. 21.

CONCORDANCE: Kargel & Lais 1578₅, fol. D3v, no. 21.

ATTRIBUTION: none.

INTABULATOR: Sixt Kargel.

VOCAL MODEL: see no. [1].

CRITICAL NOTES: M. 5, chord 1, note 4, *2* on e′ string—*3* supplied by analogy with m. 13 and 1578 reprint. M. 6, chord 2 lacks semiminim rhythm symbol—supplied from 1578 reprint. M. 15, last note, *3* on e′ string—*5* supplied from vocal model and 1578 reprint. M. 29, chord 2, note 2, *5* on g string—*2* supplied by analogy with m. 34—note 3, *3* on d′ string—*0* supplied by analogy with m. 34. M. 30, chord 1, note 4, *2* on e′ string—*3* supplied from 1578 reprint—last note, *7* on e′ string—*X* supplied by analogy with m. 25 and from 1578 reprint.

[42] *Madonna mia pietà*

SOURCE: Kargel & Lais 1578₅, fol. D2, no. 19.

CONCORDANCE: Kargel & Lais 1575₃, fol. D2, no. 19.

ATTRIBUTION: none.

INTABULATOR: Sixt Kargel.

VOCAL MODEL: see no. [2].

CRITICAL NOTES: M. 14, beat 2 lacks croma rhythm symbol in 1575 edition. M. 23, beat 2, note 2, *2* on b string in 1575 edition. M. 30, chord 1, *5* on e′ string in 1575 edition.

[43] *Tu sai madonna*

SOURCE: Kargel & Lais 1578₅, fol. D3, no. 20.

CONCORDANCE: Kargel & Lais 1575₃, fol. D3, no. 20.

ATTRIBUTION: none.

INTABULATOR: Sixt Kargel.

VOCAL MODEL: see no. [5].

CRITICAL NOTES: M. 6, chord 1, note 1, *0* on g string in 1575 edition, note 2, *0* on d′ string in 1575 edition. M. 30, chord 1, note 4, *6* on e′ string in 1575 edition. M. 38, chord 2, note 5, *5* on e′ string in 1575 edition.

Intabulations for Keyboard

[44] *La cortesia*

SOURCE: CoimU 242, fol. 157v.

ATTRIBUTION: Orlande.

INTABULATOR: anon.

VOCAL MODEL: see no. [1].

CRITICAL NOTES: M. 29, cantus, note 4 is semiminim. M. 31, tenor, note 3 is e′.

[45] *No giorno*

SOURCE: CoimU 242, fol. 157v.

ATTRIBUTION: Orlande de Lassus.

INTABULATOR: anon.

VOCAL MODEL: see no. [3].

CRITICAL NOTES: M. 16, tenor, note 1, semiminim lacks dot, note 2, semiminim. M. 19, proportion is denoted by the numeral *3* and coloration; the return to *integer valor* at m. 22 is not indicated. M. 23, tenor, note 3, semiminim. M. 25, proportion is denoted by the numeral *3* and coloration; the return to *integer valor* at m. 28 is not indicated. Mm. 25–30, alto and tenor parts lacking—reconstructed from mm. 19–24.

Plate 1. Map of Naples, from *La città de Napoli gentile* (Rome: Claudio Duchetti, 1585).
Reproduced by permission of the Museo Nazionale di San Martino, Naples.

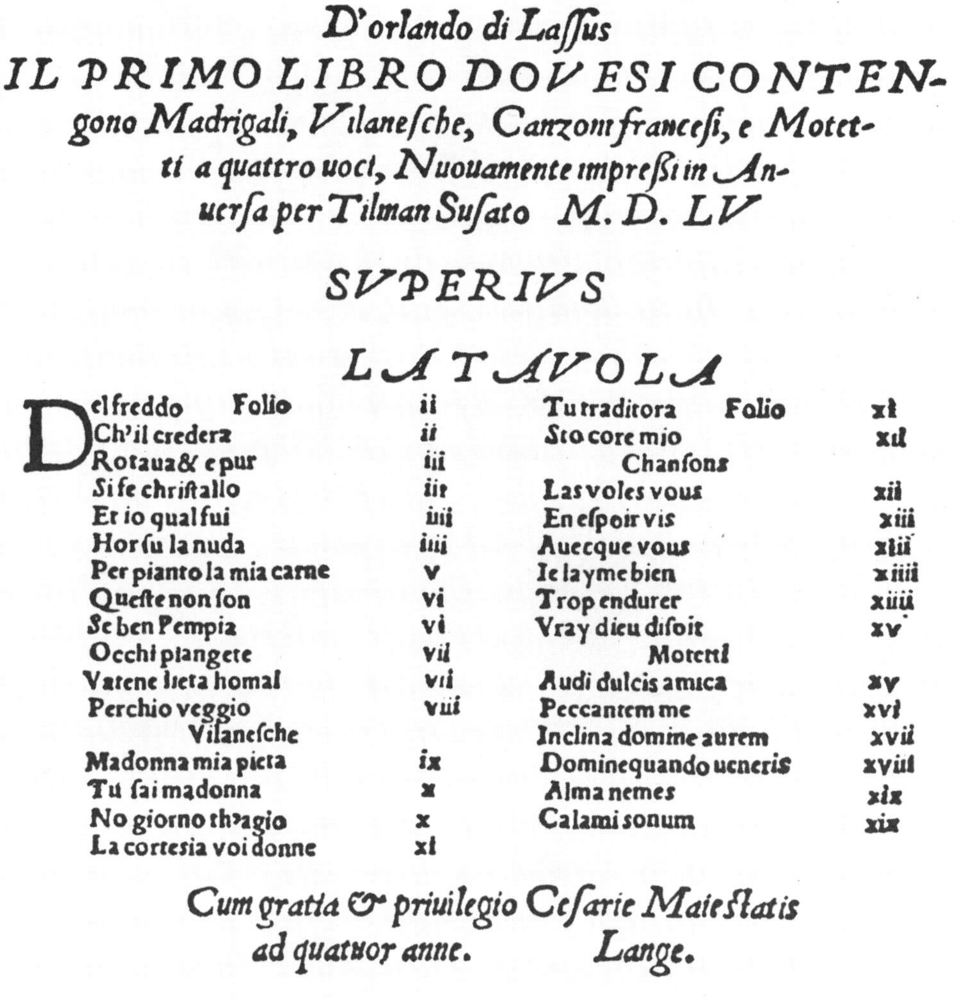

D'orlando di Lassus

IL PRIMO LIBRO DOVESI CONTEN-

gono Madrigali, Vilanesche, Canzoni francesi, e Motet-
ti a quattro uoci, Nuouamente impreßi in An-
uersa per Tilman Susato   M. D. LV

SVPERIVS

LA TAVOLA

Del freddo	Folio	ii	Tu traditora Folio	xi
Ch'il credera		ii	Sto core mio	xi
Rotaua & e pur		iii	**Chansons**	
Si fe chriftallo		iii	Las voles vous	xii
Et io qual fui		iiii	En efpoir vis	xiii
Horfu la nuda		iiii	Auecque vous	xiii
Per pianto la mia carne		v	Ie layme bien	xiiii
Quefte non fon		vi	Trop endurer	xiiii
Se ben l'empia		vi	Vray dieu difoit	xv
Occhi piangete		vii	**Motetti**	
Varene lieta homai		vii	Audi dulcis amica	xv
Perchio veggio		viii	Peccantem me	xvi
Vilanefche			Inclina domine aurem	xvii
Madonna mia pieta		ix	Domine quando ueneris	xviii
Tu fai madonna		x	Alma nemes	xix
No giorno th'agio		x	Calami sonum	xix
La cortesia voi donne		xi		

Cum gratia & priuilegio Cefarie Maieftatis
ad quatuor anne.   **Lange.**

Plate 2. Title page of the Superius partbook of Lasso's "Opus I," first edition, second issue (Antwerp: Tielman Susato, 1555). (Actual size: 15 × 21 cm.) Reproduced by permission of the Staatsbibliothek Preußischer Kulturbesitz, Musikabteilung, Berlin.

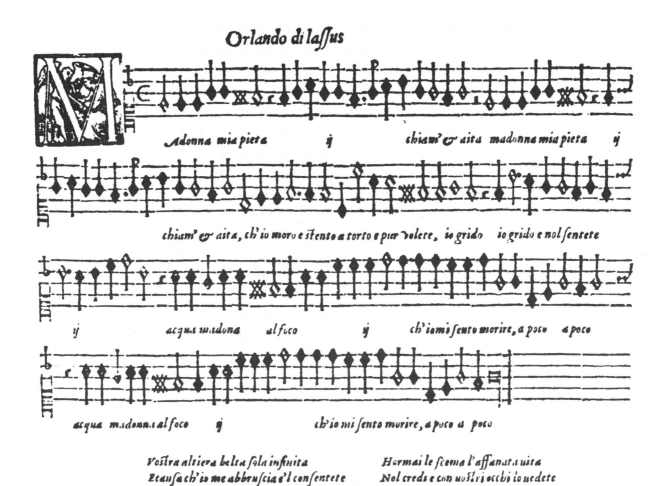

Plate 3. Orlando di Lasso, *Madonna mia, pietà*, from the Superius partbook of *Le quatoirsiesme livre a quatre parties* (Antwerp: Tielman Susato, 1555), fol. 9v. (Actual size: 15 × 21 cm.) Reproduced by permission of the Bayerische Staatsbibliothek, Munich.

Villanesche from Lasso's "Opus I" (1555)

[1] La cortesia voi donne predicate

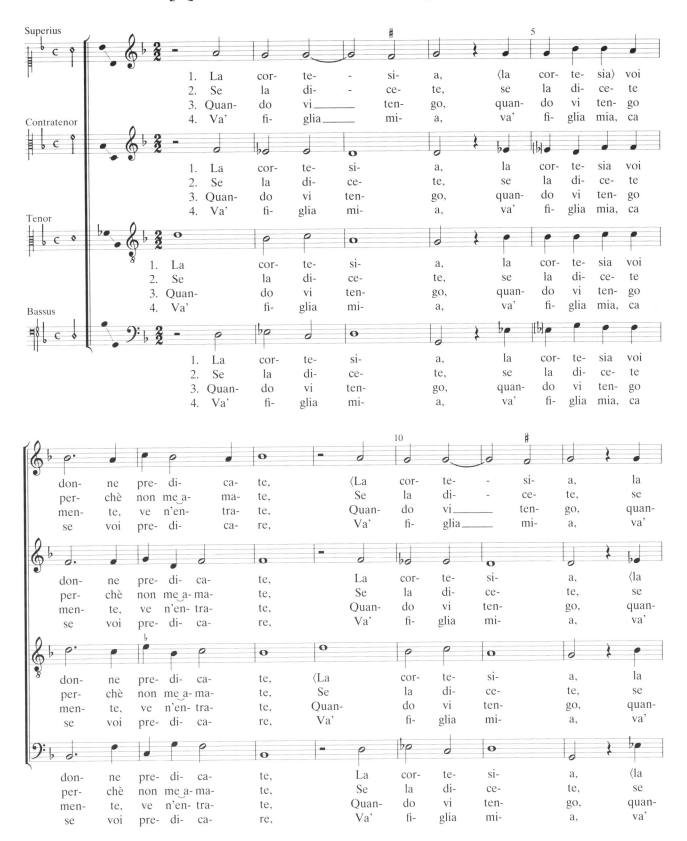

4

[2] Madonna mia, pietà chiam'et aita

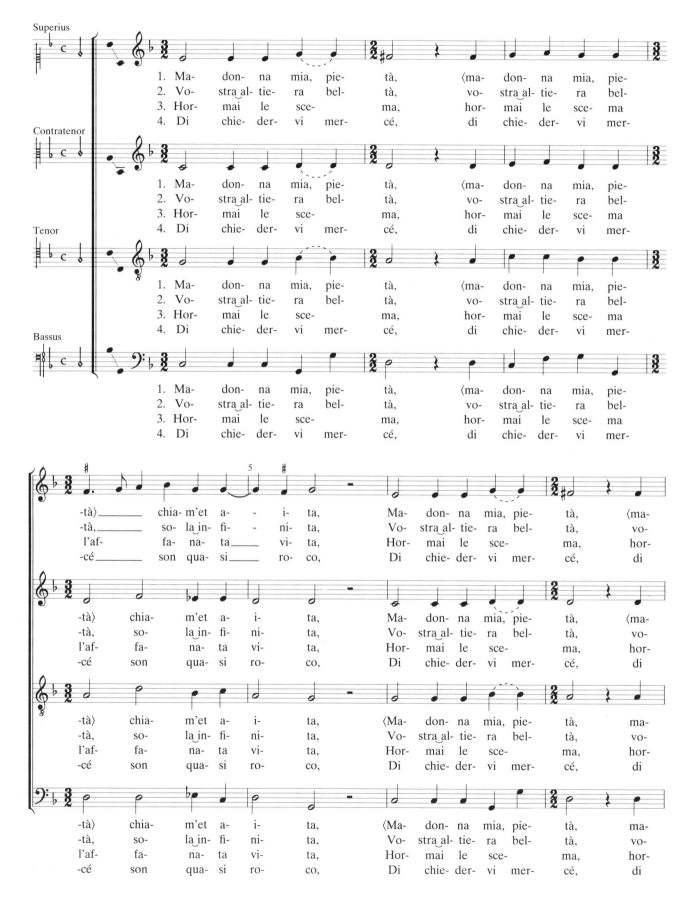

6

8

[3] 'No giorno t'haggio havere intra 'ste mane

[4] 'Sto core mio se fosse di diamante

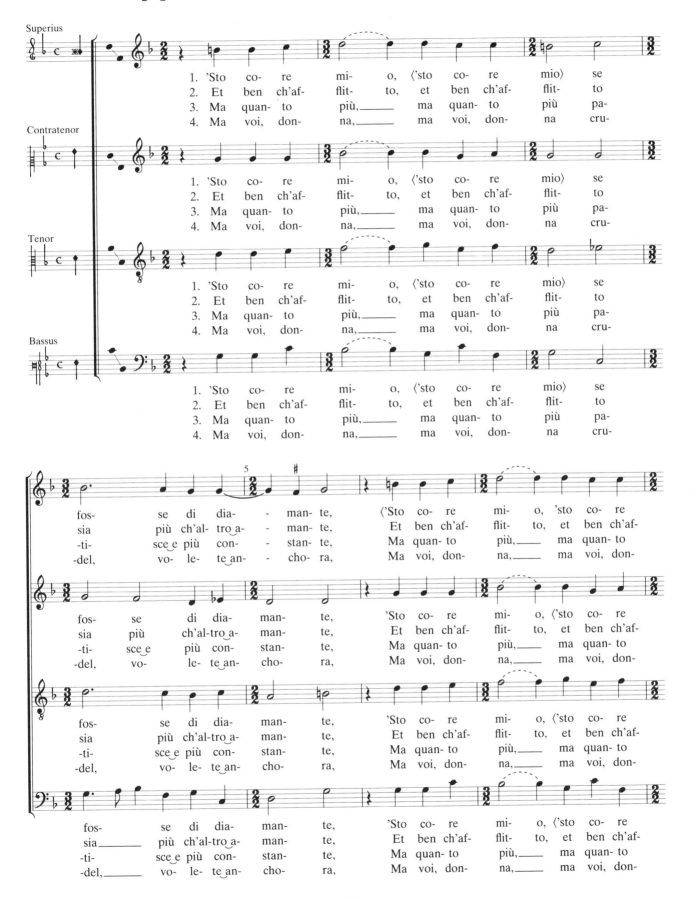

12

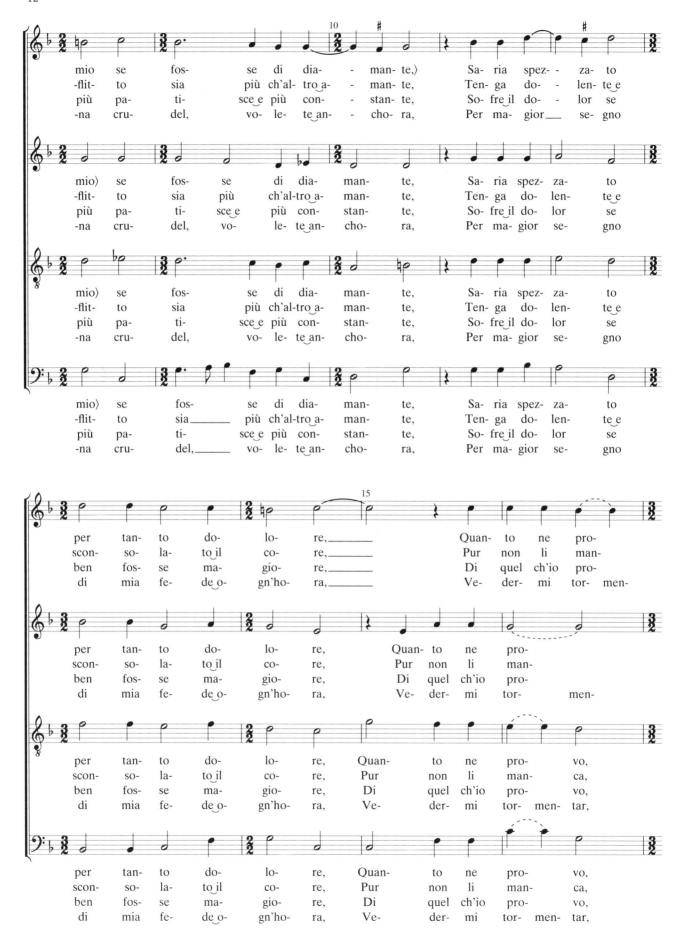

mio se fos- se di dia- man- te,⟩ Sa- ria spez- za- to
-flit- to sia più ch'al-tro a- man- te, Ten- ga do- len- te e
più pa- ti- sce e più con- stan- te, So- fre il do- lor se
-na cru- del, vo- le- te an- cho- ra, Per ma- gior___ se- gno

mio⟩ se fos- se di dia- man- te, Sa- ria spez- za- to
-flit- to sia più ch'al-tro a- man- te, Ten- ga do- len- te e
più pa- ti- sce e più con- stan- te, So- fre il do- lor se
-na cru- del, vo- le- te an- cho- ra, Per ma- gior se- gno

mio⟩ se fos- se di dia- man- te, Sa- ria spez- za- to
-flit- to sia più ch'al-tro a- man- te, Ten- ga do- len- te e
più pa- ti- sce e più con- stan- te, So- fre il do- lor se
-na cru- del, vo- le- te an- cho- ra, Per ma- gior se- gno

mio⟩ se fos- se di dia- man- te, Sa- ria spez- za- to
-flit- to sia_____ più ch'al-tro a- man- te, Ten- ga do- len- te e
più pa- ti- sce e più con- stan- te, So- fre il do- lor se
-na cru- del,_____ vo- le- te an- cho- ra, Per ma- gior se- gno

per tan- to do- lo- re,_____ Quan- to ne pro- vo,
scon- so- la- to il co- re,_____ Pur non li man- ca,
ben fos- se ma- gio- re,_____ Di quel ch'io pro- vo,
di mia fe- de o- gn'ho- ra,_____ Ve- der- mi tor- men-

per tan- to do- lo- re, Quan- to ne pro- vo,
scon- so- la- to il co- re, Pur non li man- ca,
ben fos- se ma- gio- re, Di quel ch'io pro- vo,
di mia fe- de o- gn'ho- ra, Ve- der- mi tor- men-

per tan- to do- lo- re, Quan- to ne pro- vo,
scon- so- la- to il co- re, Pur non li man- ca,
ben fos- se ma- gio- re, Di quel ch'io pro- vo,
di mia fe- de o- gn'ho- ra, Ve- der- mi tor- men- tar,

per tan- to do- lo- re, Quan- to ne pro- vo,
scon- so- la- to il co- re, Pur non li man- ca,
ben fos- se ma- gio- re, Di quel ch'io pro- vo,
di mia fe- de o- gn'ho- ra, Ve- der- mi tor- men- tar,

[5] Tu sai, madonna mia, ch'io t'amo et voglio

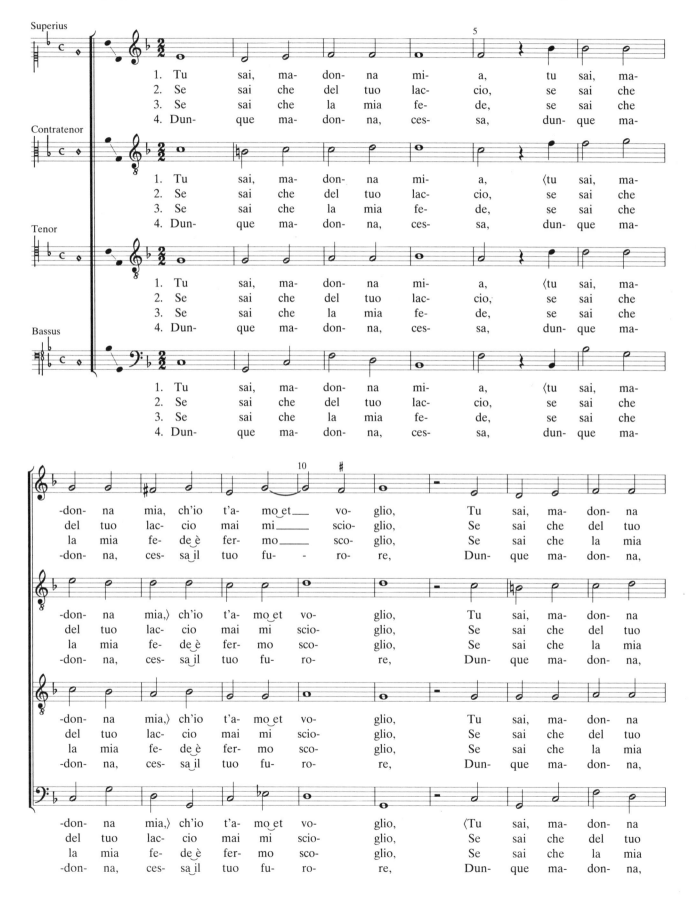

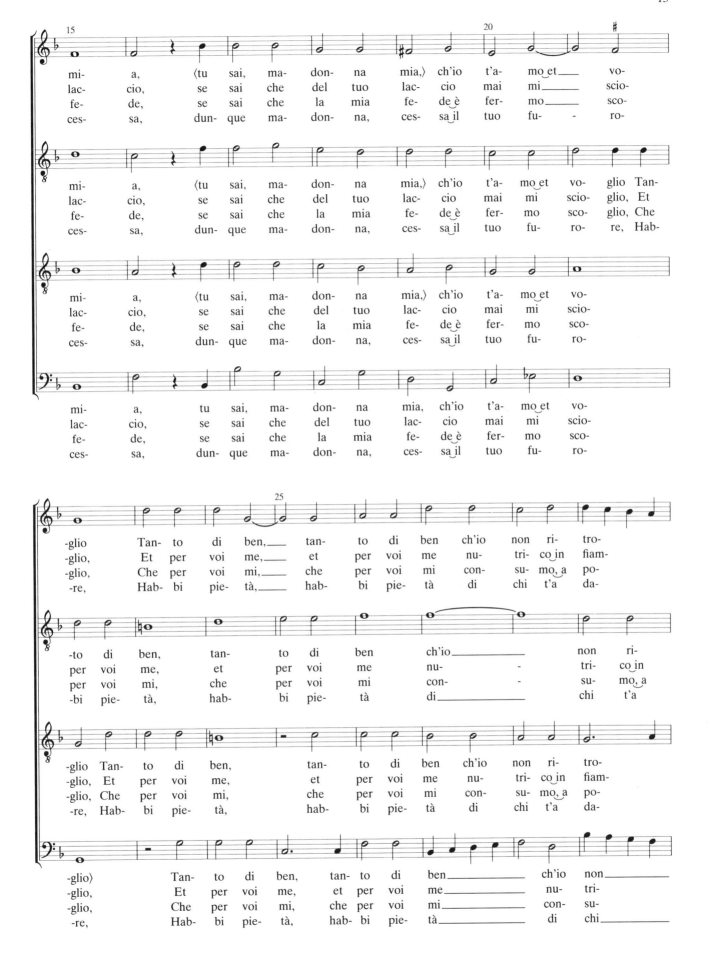

18

[6] Tu, traditora, m'hai puost'a 'sto core

Neapolitan Models for Lasso's *Villanesche*

[7] La cortesia voi donne predicate

Vicenzo Fontana

1. La   cor- te- si-   a,   la   cor- te- sia   voi
2. Se   la   di- ce-   te,   se   la   di- ce-   te
3. Quan- do   ve   ten-   go,   quan- do   ve   ten- go
4. Va'   fi-   glia   mi-   a,   va'   fi-   glia   mia,   ca

don-   ne   pre- di- ca-   te,   La   cor- te- si-   a,   la
per-   chè   non me_a- ma-   te,   Se   la   di- ce-   te,   se
men-   te,   ve   n'en- tra-   te,   Quan- do   ve   ten-   go,   quan- va'
se   voi   pre- di- ca-   re,   Va'   fi-   glia   mi-   a,   va'

cor- te- sia voi don- ne pre- di- ca- te, Ma ma- i, ma ma- i, ma
la di- ce- te per- chè non me a- ma- te, Et ha- i, et ha- i, et
-do ve ten- go men- te, ve n'en- tra- te, E sen- za, e sen- za, e
fi- glia mia, ca se voi pre- di- ca- re, L'o- pe- re, l'o- pe- re, l'o-

cor- te- sia voi don- ne pre- di- ca- te, Ma ma- i, ma ma- i, ma
la di- ce- te per- chè non me a- ma- te, Et ha- i, et ha- i, et
-do ve ten- go men- te, ve n'en- tra- te, E sen- za, e sen- za, e
fi- glia mia, ca se voi pre- di- ca- re, L'o- pe- re, l'o- pe- re, l'o-

cor- te- sia voi don- ne pre- di- ca- te, Ma ma- i, ma ma- i, ma
la di- ce- te per- chè non me a- ma- te, Et ha- i, et ha- i, et
-do ve ten- go men- te, ve n'en- tra- te, E sen- za, e sen- za, e
fi- glia mia, ca se voi pre- di- ca- re, L'o- pe- re, l'o- pe- re, l'o-

mai non l'os- ser- va- te, vi so di- re. 1–4. *Voi lo ve- de- te s'è*
hai pie- tà di tan- to mio mar- ti- re. 1–4. *Voi lo ve- de- te s'è*
sen- za cau- sa me voi far mo- ri- re. 1–4. *Voi lo ve- de- te s'è*
-pe- re bo- ne ti bi- so- gna fa- re.

mai non l'os- ser- va- te, vi so di- re. 1–4. *Voi lo ve- de- te s'è*
hai pie- tà di tan- to mio mar- ti- re.
sen- za cau- sa me voi far mo- ri- re.
-pe- re bo- ne ti bi- so- gna fa- re.

mai non l'os- ser- va- te, vi so di- re. 1–4. *Voi lo ve- de- te s'è*
hai pie- tà di tan- to mio mar- ti- re.
sen- za cau- sa me voi far mo- ri- re.
-pe- re bo- ne ti bi- so- gna fa- re.

[8] Madonna mia, pietà chiam'et aita

Vicenzo Fontana

24

[9] 'No giorno t'hagio havere intra 'ste mane

Vicenzo Fontana

28

1–4. Fug- gi- mi, ⟨fug- gi- mi,⟩ fug- gi- mi quan- to voi, che non mi scap- pi,

1–4. Fug- gi- mi, ⟨fug- gi- mi,⟩ fug- gi- mi quan-to voi, che non mi scap- pi,

1–4. Fug- gi- mi, ⟨fug- gi- mi,⟩ fug- gi- mi quan-to voi, che non mi scap- pi,

Fug- gi- mi, ⟨fug- gi- mi,⟩ fug- gi- mi quan- to voi, che non mi scap- pi.

Fug- gi- mi, ⟨fug- gi- mi,⟩ fug- gi- mi quan-to voi, che non mi scap- pi.

Fug- gi- mi, ⟨fug- gi- mi,⟩ fug- gi- mi quan-to voi, che non mi scap- pi.

[10] 'Sto core mio se fusse de diamante

[Anon.]

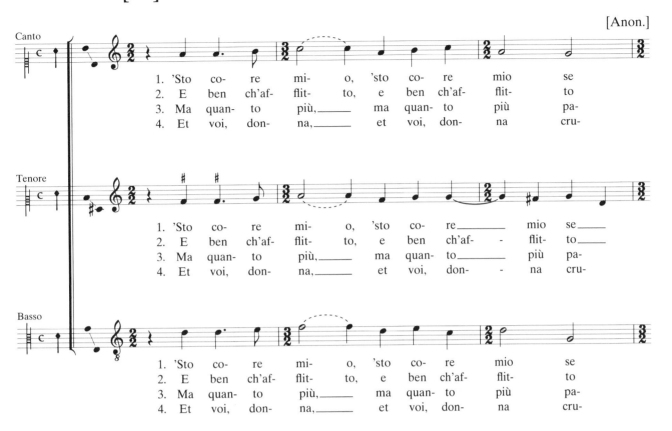

Quan- to ne pro- vo, quan- to ne pro- v'e sen- t'a___ tut- te l'ho- re.
Non le man-cha nè, non le man-cha nè for- za___ nè vi- go- re.
Di quel ch'io sen- to, di quel ch'io sen-to et pro- v'a tut- te l'ho- re.
Ve- der-mi tor-men- tar, ve- der-mi tor- men- tar pri- ma ch'io mo- ra.

-to ne pro- v'e sen- to, quan- to ne pro- v'e sen- t'a tut- te_____ l'ho- re.
le man-cha nè for- za, non le man-cha nè for- za nè vi- go- re.
quel ch'io sen-to et pro- vo, di quel ch'io sen-to et pro- v'a tut- te_____ l'ho- re.
-der-mi tor-men- tar,___ ve- der-mi tor-men- tar pri- ma ch'io___ mo- ra.

-to ne pro- v'e sen- to, quan- to ne pro- v'e sen- t'a tut- te l'ho- re.
le man-cha nè for- za, non le man-ca nè for- za nè vi- go- re.
quel ch'io sen-to et pro- vo, di quel ch'io sen-to et pro- v'a tut- te l'ho- re.
-der-mi tor-men- tar, ve- der-mi tor-men- tar pri- ma ch'io mo- ra.

[11] Tu sai, madonna mia, ch'io t'amo e voglio

Vicenzo Fontana

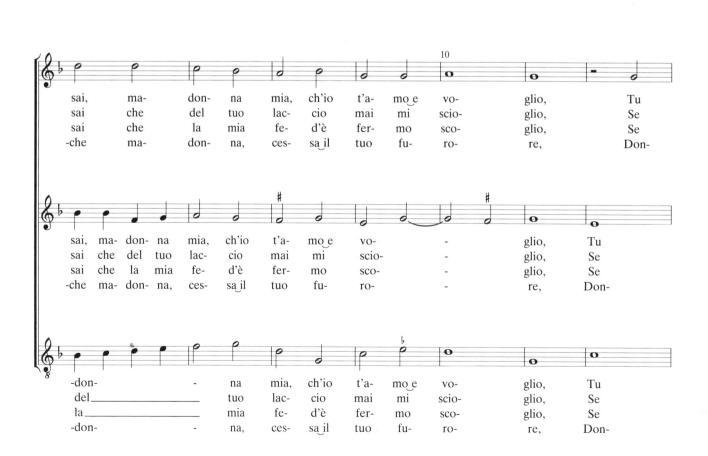

Villanelle from Lasso's *Libro de villanelle* (1581)
[12] Ad altre le voi dare 'ste passate

[13] Ecco la nimph'Ebrayca chiamata

[14] Io ti voria contar la pena mia

Canto
Io ti vo- ria con- tar la pe- na mi- a,
Io ⟨ti vo- ria con- tar la pe- na mi- a,⟩ Ma non ce ba- sta-
-ria- no mil- le me- si, ⟨Ma non ce ba- sta- ria- no mil- le me- si.⟩ Ti

Alto
Io ti vo- ria con- tar la pe- na mi- a,
Io ⟨ti vo- ria con- tar la pe- na mi- a,⟩ Ma non ce ba- sta-
-ria- no mil- le me- si, ⟨Ma non ce ba- sta- ria- no mil- le me- si.⟩ Ti

Tenore
Io ti vo- ria con- tar la pe- na mi- a,
Io ⟨ti vo- ria con- tar la pe- na mi- a,⟩ Ma non ce ba- sta-
-ria- no mil- le me- si, ⟨Ma non ce ba- sta- ria- no mil- le me- si.⟩ Ti

Basso
Io ti vo- ria con- tar la pe- na mi- a,
Io ⟨ti vo- ria con- tar la pe- na mi- a,⟩ Ma non ce ba- sta-
-ria- no mil- le me- si, ⟨Ma non ce ba- sta- ria- no mil- le me- si.⟩ Ti

44

[15] O belle, fusa! chi ne vo' accatare?

Canto
O bel- le, fu- sa! 〈o bel- le, fu-

Alto
O, o bel- le, fu- sa! 〈o bel- le, fu-

Tenore
O bel- le, fu- sa! 〈o bel- le, fu- sa!〉

Basso
O bel- le, fu- sa! 〈o bel- le, fu- sa!〉

-sa!〉 o bel- le, fu- sa! chi ne vo'_ac- ca- ta- re? O bel- le,

-sa!〉 o bel- le, fu- sa! chi ne vo'_ac- ca- ta- re? O, o

o bel- le, fu- sa! chi ne vo'_ac- ca- ta- re? O bel- le,

o bel- le, fu- sa! chi ne vo'_ac- ca- ta- re? O bel- le,

fu- sa! 〈o bel- le, fu- sa!〉 o bel- le, fu-

bel- le, fu- sa! 〈o bel- le, fu- sa!〉 o bel- le, fu-

fu- sa! 〈o bel- le, fu- sa!〉 o bel- le, fu- sa!

fu- sa! 〈o bel- le, fu- sa!〉 o bel- le, fu- sa!

46

[16] O occhi manza mia, cigli dorati

[17] Ogni giorno m'han ditt'a chi favelli

[18] Par ch'hai lasciato de non t'affacciare

con te sa- pe lo Don Die- go, lo Don Die- go, lo Don Die- go.

con te sa- pe lo Don Die- go, lo Don Die- go, lo Don Die- go.

con te sa- pe lo Don Die- go, lo Don Die- go, lo Don Die- go.

con te sa- pe lo Don Die- go, lo Don Die- go, lo Don Die- go.

2. For- se te cre... for- - se te cre- di di me la- ni- a- re,

2. For- se te cre... for- - se te cre- di di me la- ni- a- re,

2. For- se te cre... for- - se te cre- di di me la- ni- a- re,

2. For- se te cre... for- - se te cre- di di me la- ni- a- re,

Che me stà in- chiu- sa co- me stes- s'in cel- la, co- me stes- s'in cel- la.

Che me stà in- chiu- sa co- me stes- s'in cel- la, co- me stes- s'in cel- la.

Che me stà in- chiu- sa co- me stes- s'in cel- la, co- me stes- s'in cel- la.

Che me stà in- chiu- sa co- me stes- s'in cel- la, co- me stes- s'in cel- la.

Deh, po- ve- rel- la con tan- to su- sie- go, Non far che

Deh, po- ve- rel- la con tan- to su- sie- go, Non far che

Deh, po- ve- rel- la con tan- to su- sie- go, Non far che

Deh, po- ve- rel- la con tan- to su- sie- go, Non far che

con te sa- pe lo Don Die- go, lo Don Die- go, lo Don Die- go.

con te sa- pe lo Don Die- go, lo Don Die- go, lo Don Die- go.

con te sa- pe lo Don Die- go, lo Don Die- go, lo Don Die- go.

con te sa- pe lo Don Die- go, lo Don Die- go, lo Don Die- go.

3. Ti- ra, ti- ra, ti- ra, ti- ra, ti- ra, ti- ra, cà te dov- ris- si ver- go-

3. Ti- ra, ti- ra, ti- ra, ti- ra, ti- ra, ti- ra, cà te dov- ris- si ver- go-

3. Ti- ra, ti- ra, ti- ra, ti- ra, ti- ra, ti- ra, cà te dov- ris- si ver- go-

3. Ti- ra, ti- ra, ti- ra, ti- ra, ti- ra, ti- ra, cà te dov- ris- si ver- go-

58

[19] Saccio 'na cosa ch'è di legn'e tonda

vol- ta,⟩ ch'è strom-bo- lo che vol- t'o ar- ga- - tel- la, Ch'è strom-bo- lo che

vol- ta,⟩ ch'è strom-bo- lo che vol- t'o ar- ga- tel- la, Ch'è strom-bo- lo che

vol- ta,⟩ ch'è strom-bo- lo che vol- t'o ar- ga- tel- la, Ch'è strom-bo- lo che

vol- ta,⟩ ch'è strom-bo- lo che vol- t'o ar- ga- tel- la, Ch'è strom-bo- lo che

vol- ta, ch'è ⟨strom-bo- lo che vol- ta,⟩ ch'è strom-bo- lo che vol- t'o ar- ga- - tel- la.

vol- ta, ch'è ⟨strom-bo- lo che vol- ta,⟩ ch'è strom-bo- lo che vol- t'o ar- ga- tel- la.

vol- ta, ⟨ch'è strom-bo- lo che vol- ta,⟩ ch'è strom-bo- lo che vol- t'o ar- ga- tel- la.

vol- ta, ch'è ⟨strom-bo- lo che vol- ta,⟩ ch'è strom-bo- lo che vol- t'o ar- ga- tel- la.

[20] S'io fusse ciaul'et tu lo campanile

[21] S'io ti vedess'una sol volt'il giorno

-ten- to ne sta- ria⟩ tut- ta la____ se- ra. Fa ru re ra, ⟨fa ru

-ten- to ne sta- ria⟩ tut- ta la se- ra. Fa ru re ra, ⟨fa ru

-ten- to ne sta- ria⟩_____ tut- ta la se- ra. Fa ru re ra, ⟨fa ru

-ten- to ne sta- ria⟩ tut- ta la se- ra. Fa ru re ra, ⟨fa ru

re ra,⟩ fa ru re ra, Bel- la fior di pri- ma- ve- ra.

re ra,⟩ fa ru re ra, Bel- la fior di pri- ma- ve- ra.

re ra,⟩ fa ru re ra, Bel- la fior di pri- ma- ve- ra.

re ra,⟩ fa ru re ra, Bel- la fior di pri- ma- ve- ra.

[22] S'io ve dico ca sete la chiù bella

-co lo ve- r'e voi,⟩ di- co lo ve- r'e voi ve ne sde- - gna- te.

-co lo ve- r'e voi,⟩ di- co lo ve- r'e voi ve ne sde- gna- te.

ve- r'e voi,⟩ di- co lo ve- r'e voi ve ne sde- gna- te.

-co lo ve- r'e voi,⟩ di- co lo ve- r'e voi ve ne sde- gna- te.

[23] Tutto lo dì mi dici, "canta, canta"

74

Neapolitan Models for Lasso's *Villanelle*

[24] Ad altre lo voi dare 'ste passate

Don Ioan Domenico del Giovane de Nola

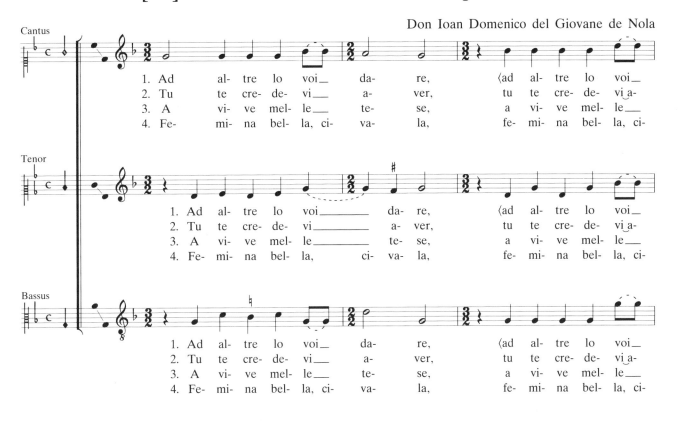

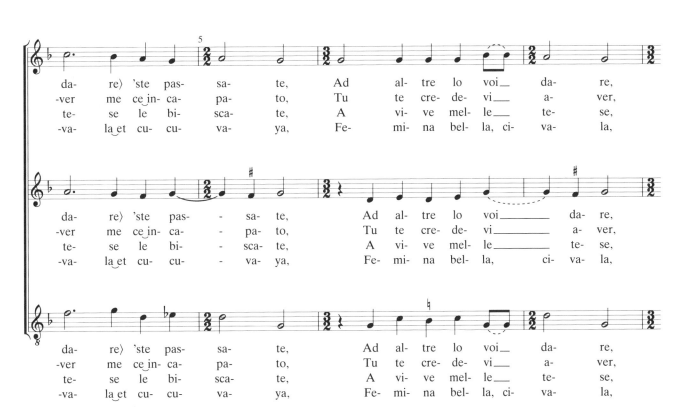

[25] Ecco la nimph'Ebraica chiamata

Don Ioan Domenico del Giovane de Nola

[26] O belle, fusa! chi ne vo' accatare?

Don Ioan Domenico del Giovane de Nola

[27] O occhi manza mia, cigli dorati

[Anon.]

Canto

1. O oc- chi man- za mi- a, o oc- chi man- za
2. O boc- ca co- me zuc- ca- ro, o boc- ca co- me
3. O piet- to che con- for- ti, o piet- to che con-
4. Per tan- te quan- te gra- ti- e, per tan- te quan- te

Tenore

1. O oc- chi man- za mi- a, o oc- chi man- za
2. O boc- ca co- me zuc- ca- ro, o boc- ca co- me
3. O piet- to che con- for- ti, o piet- to che con-
4. Per tan- te quan- te gra- ti- e, per tan- te quan- te

Basso

1. O oc- chi man- za mi- a, o oc- chi man- za
2. O boc- ca co- me zuc- ca- ro, o boc- ca co- me
3. O piet- to che con- for- ti, o piet- to che con-
4. Per tan- te quan- te gra- ti- e, per tan- te quan- te

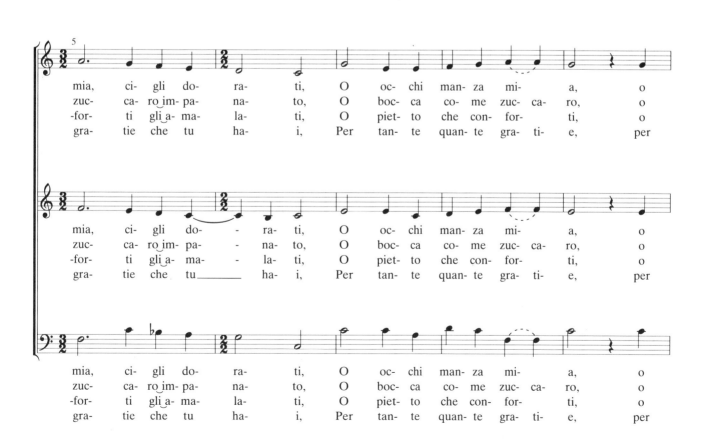

5

mia, ci- gli do- ra- ti, O oc- chi man- za mi- a, o
zuc- ca- ro im- pa- na- to, O boc- ca co- me zuc- ca- ro, o
-for- ti gli a- ma- la- ti, O piet- to che con- for- ti, o
gra- tie che tu ha- i, Per tan- te quan- te gra- ti- e, per

mia, ci- gli do- ra- ti, O oc- chi man- za mi- a, o
zuc- ca- ro im- pa- na- to, O boc- ca co- me zuc- ca- ro, o
-for- ti gli a- ma- la- ti, O piet- to che con- for- ti, o
gra- tie che tu____ ha- i, Per tan- te quan- te gra- ti- e, per

mia, ci- gli do- ra- ti, O oc- chi man- za mi- a, o
zuc- ca- ro im- pa- na- to, O boc- ca co- me zuc- ca- ro, o
-for- ti gli a- ma- la- ti, O piet- to che con- for- ti, o
gra- tie che tu ha- i, Per tan- te quan- te gra- ti- e, per

oc- chi man- za mia, ci- gli do- ra- ti, O fac- cia d'u- na
boc- ca co- me zuc- ca- ro im- pa- na- to, O can- na che spec-
piet- to che con- for- ti gli a- ma- la- ti, Pie- no di fio- ri et
tan- te quan- te gra- tie che tu ha- i, Ri- cor- da- ti

oc- chi man- za mia, ci- gli do- ra- ti, O fac- cia d'u- na___
boc- ca co- me zuc- ca- ro im- pa- na- to, O can- na che___ spec-
piet- to che con- for- ti gli a- ma- la- ti, Pie- no di fio- ri et___
tan- te quan- te gra- tie che tu___ ha- i, Ri- cor- da- ti___

oc- chi man- za mia, ci- gli do- ra- ti, O fac- cia d'u- na
boc- ca co- me zuc- ca- ro im- pa- na- to, O can- na che spec-
piet- to che con- for- ti gli a- ma- la- ti, Pie- no di fio- ri et
tan- te quan- te gra- tie che tu ha- i, Ri- cor- da- ti

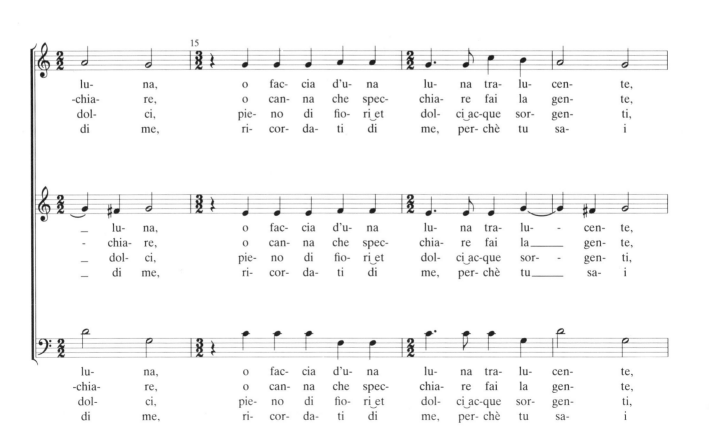

lu- na, o fac- cia d'u- na lu- na tra lu- cen- te,
-chia- re, o can- na che spec- chia- re fai la gen- te,
dol- ci, pie- no di fio- ri et dol- ci ac- que sor- gen- ti,
di me, ri- cor- da- ti di me, per- chè tu sa- i

_ lu- na, o fac- cia d'u- na lu- na tra lu- cen- te,
- chia- re, o can- na che spec- chia- re fai la___ gen- te,
_ dol- ci, pie- no di fio- ri et dol- ci ac- que sor- gen- ti,
_ di me, ri- cor- da- ti di me, per- chè tu___ sa- i

lu- na, o fac- cia d'u- na lu- na tra lu- cen- te,
-chia- re, o can- na che spec- chia- re fai la gen- te,
dol- ci, pie- no di fio- ri et dol- ci ac- que sor- gen- ti,
di me, ri- cor- da- ti di me, per- chè tu sa- i

[28] Sacio 'na cosa ch'è di legno e tonda

Vicenzo Fontana

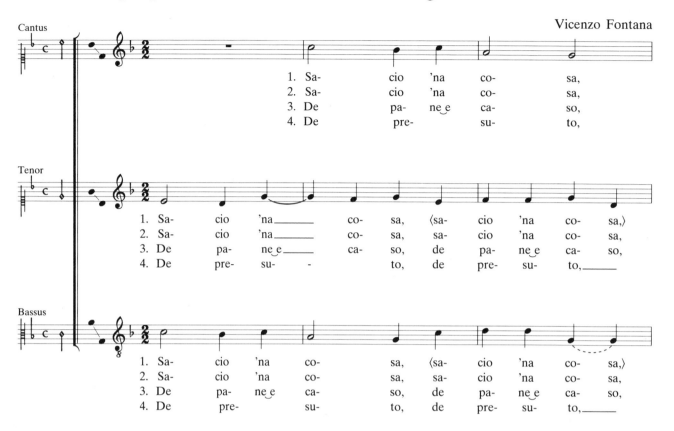

Cantus

1. Sa- cio 'na co- sa,
2. Sa- cio 'na co- sa,
3. De pa- ne e ca- so,
4. De pre- su- to,

Tenor

1. Sa- cio 'na co- sa, ⟨sa- cio 'na co- sa,⟩
2. Sa- cio 'na co- sa, sa- cio 'na co- sa,
3. De pa- ne e ca- so, de pa- ne e ca- so,
4. De pre- su- to, de pre- su- to,

Bassus

1. Sa- cio 'na co- sa, ⟨sa- cio 'na co- sa,⟩
2. Sa- cio 'na co- sa, sa- cio 'na co- sa,
3. De pa- ne e ca- so, de pa- ne e ca- so,
4. De pre- su- to, de pre- su- to,

sa- cio 'na co- sa ch'è di le- gno e ton- da, ch'è di le- gno e
sa- cio 'na co- sa e se u- sa in tut- to il mon- do, u- sa in tut- to il
de pa- ne e ca- so fus- se pe- pe fon- do, fus- se pe- pe
de pre- su- to de por- co ben tri- dat- ta, por- co ben tri-

sa- cio 'na co- sa ch'è di le- gno e ton- da, ch'è di le- gno e
sa- cio 'na co- sa e se u- sa in tut- to il mon- do, u- sa in tut- to il
de pa- ne e ca- so fus- se pe- pe fon- do, fus- se pe- pe
de pre- su- to de por- co ben tri- dat- ta, por- co ben tri-

sa- cio 'na co- sa ch'è di le- gno e ton- da, ch'è di le- gno e
sa- cio 'na co- sa e se u- sa in tut- to il mon- do, u- sa in tut- to il
de pa- ne e ca- so fus- se pe- pe fon- do, fus- se pe- pe
de pre- su- to de por- co ben tri- dat- ta, por- co ben tri-

89

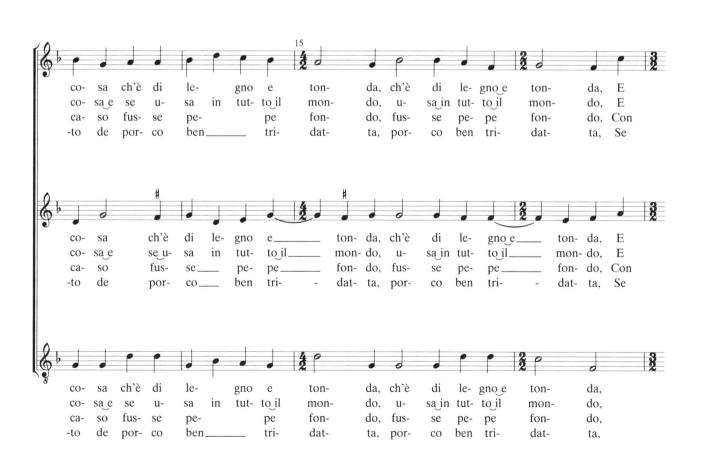

90

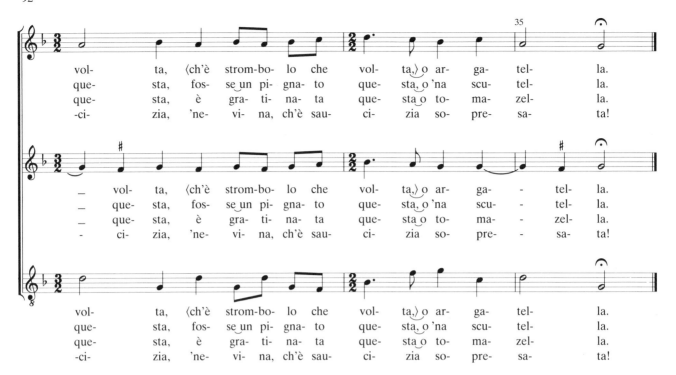

volta, ⟨ch'è strom-bo-lo che volta,⟩ o ar- ga- tel- la.
que-sta, fos-se un pi- gna- to que-sta, o 'na scu- tel- la.
que-sta, è gra- ti- na- ta que-sta o to- ma- zel- la.
-ci- zia, 'ne- vi- na, ch'è sau- ci- zia so- pre- sa- ta!

volta, ⟨ch'è strom-bo-lo che volta,⟩ o ar- tel- la.
que-sta, fos-se un pi- gna- to que-sta, o 'na scu- tel- la.
que-sta, è gra- ti- na- ta que-sta o to- ma- zel- la.
-ci- zia, 'ne- vi- na, ch'è sau- ci- zia so- pre- sa- ta!

vol-ta, ⟨ch'è strom-bo-lo che vol-ta,⟩ o ar- ga- tel- la.
que-sta, fos-se un pi- gna- to que-sta, o 'na scu- tel- la.
que-sta, è gra- ti- na- ta que-sta o to- ma- zel- la.
-ci- zia, 'ne- vi- na, ch'è sau- ci- zia so- pre- sa- ta!

Intabulations for Lute

[29] La cortesia

Orlando [di Lasso]
[Sixt Kargel]

Tuning: G c f a d' g'

94

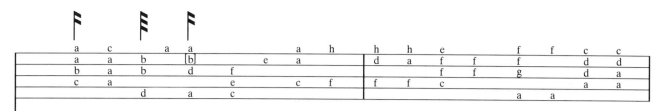

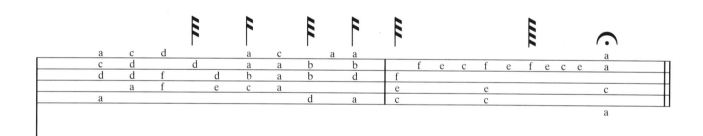

[30] Madonna mia pietà

[Orlando di Lasso]
[Sixt Kargel]

Tuning: G c f a d' g'

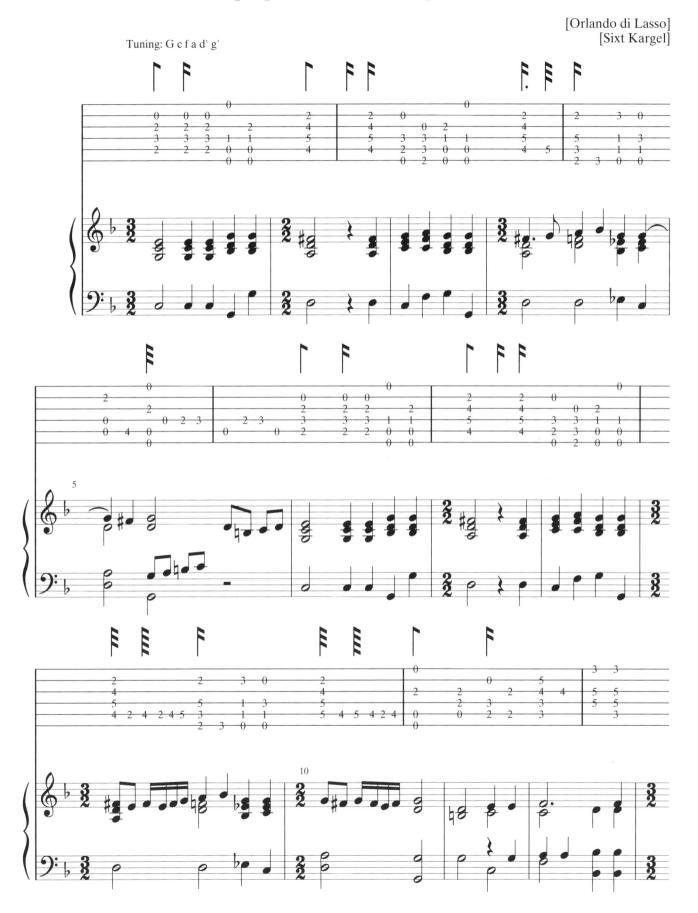

[31] Madonna mia pietà

[Orlando di Lasso]
[Emanuel Adriansen]

110

112

[32] Madonna mia pietà

[Orlando di Lasso]
[Emanuel Adriansen]

Ma- don- na mia pie- tà, ⟨ma- don- na mia pie-

Ma- don- na mia pie- tà, ⟨ma- don- na mia pie-

Tuning: G c f a d' g'

-tà⟩_____ chia-m'et a- i- ta, Ma- don- na mia pie-

-tà⟩ chia- m'et a- i- ta, Ma- don- na mia pie-

114

116

[33] Sto core mio

Orlando [di Lasso]
[Sixt Kargel]

Tuning: G c f a d' g'

[34] Tu sai madona

Orlando [di Lasso]
[Sixt Kargel]

Tuning: G c f a d' g'

122

[35] Tu traditore

Orlando [di Lasso]
[Sixt Kargel]

Tuning: G c f a d' g'

Intabulations for Four-Course Cittern

[36] La cortesia

[Orlando di Lasso]
[Anon.]

[37] Madona mia pietà

[Orlando di Lasso]
[Anon.]

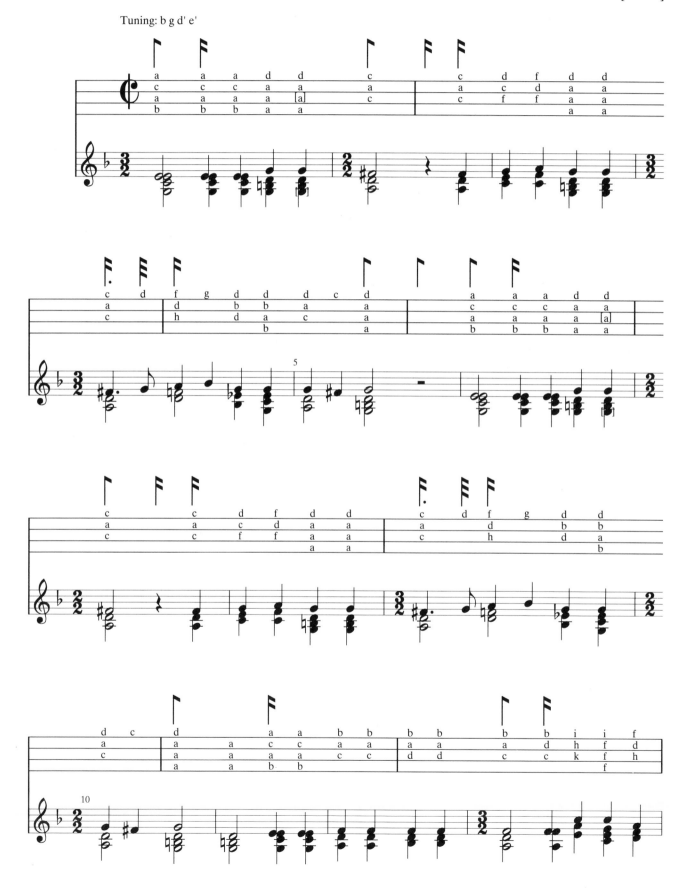

130

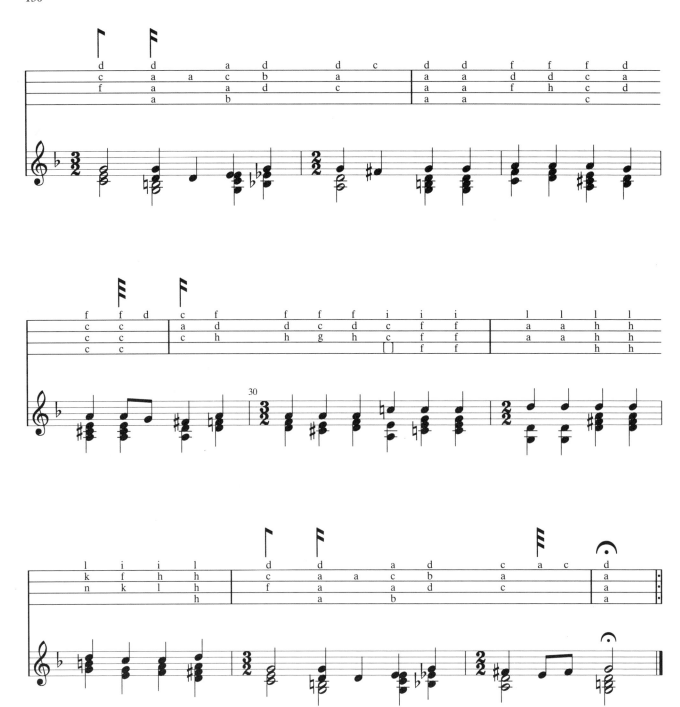

[38] Madonna mia pietà

[Orlando di Lasso]
[Sixt Kargel]

Tuning: a g d' e'

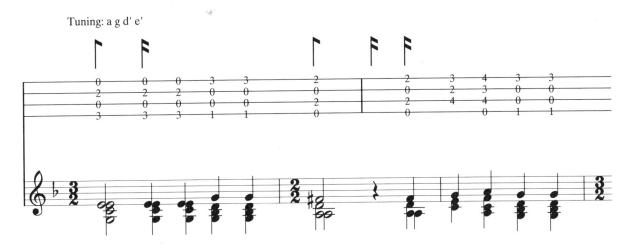

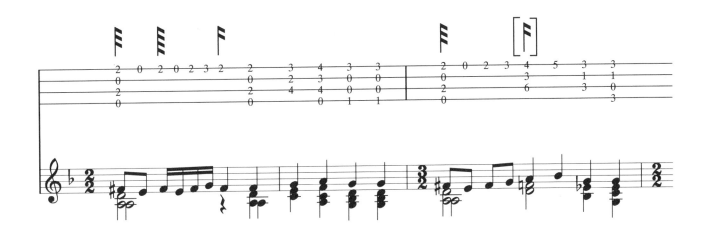

132

[39] Sto core mio

[Orlando di Lasso]
[Anon.]

Tuning: a g d' e'

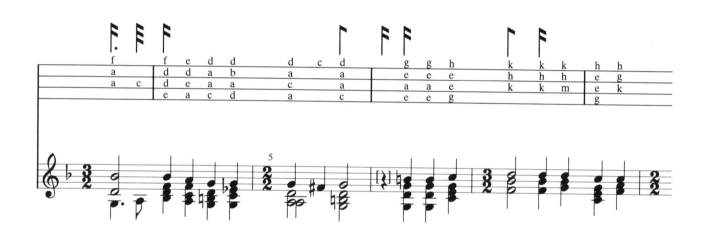

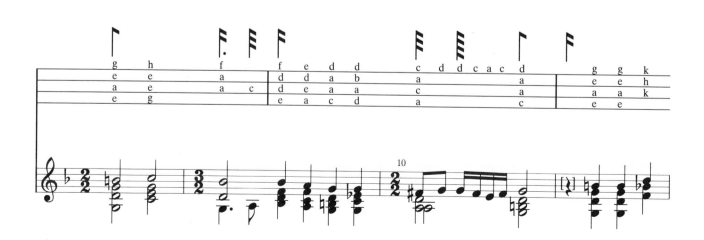

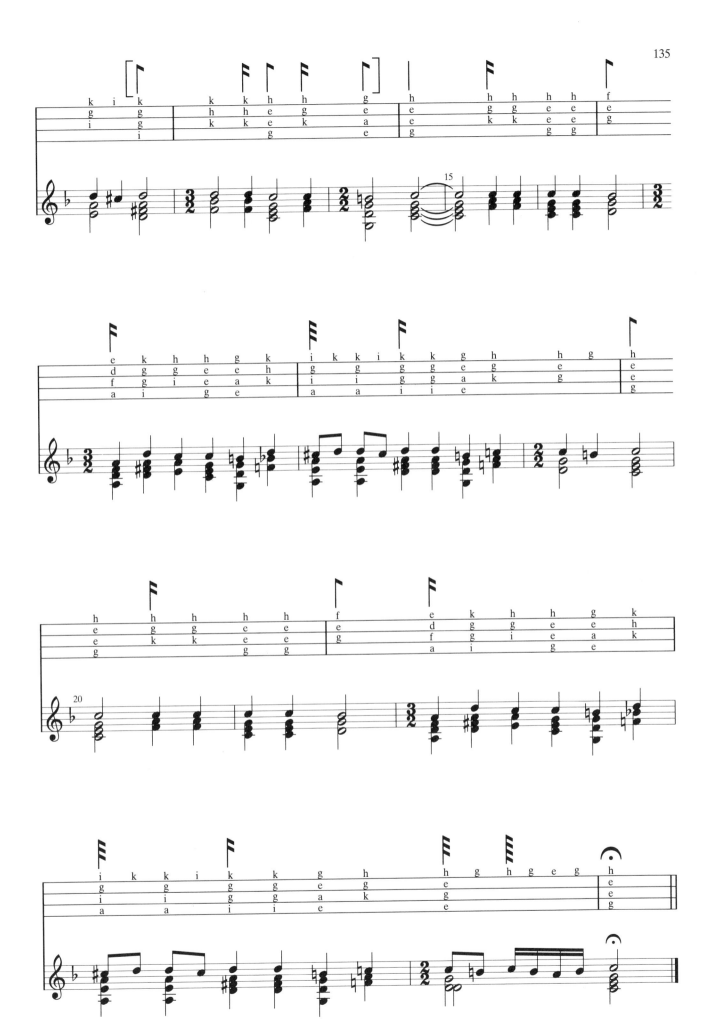

[40] Tu traditora

[Orlando di Lasso]
[Anon.]

Tuning: b g d' e'

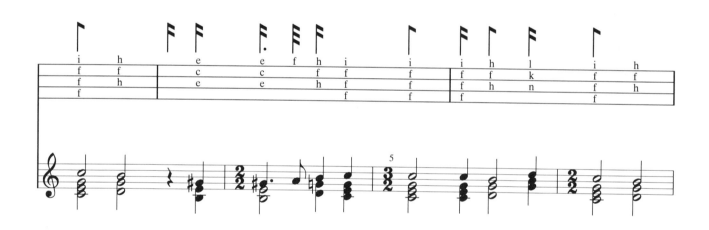

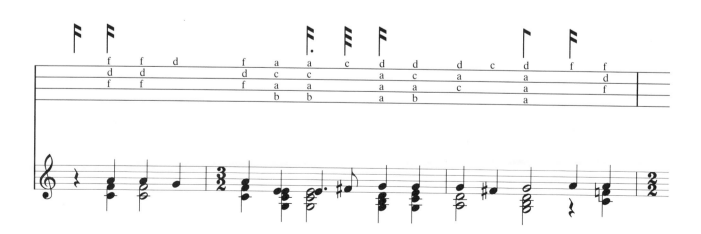

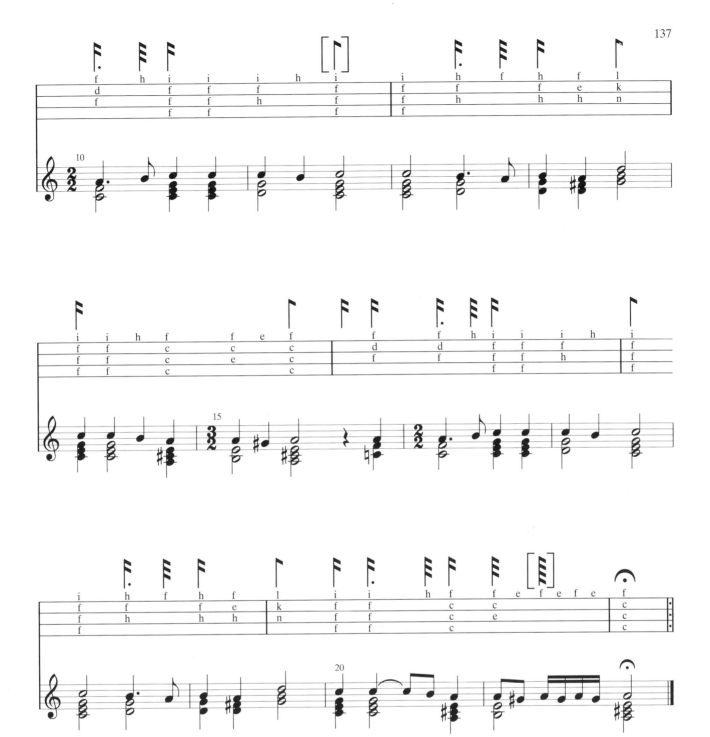

Intabulations for Six-Course Cittern

[41] La cortesia

[Orlando di Lasso]
[Sixt Kargel]

Tuning: bB gG dD gG d'd' e'e'

[42] Madonna mia pietà

[Orlando di Lasso]
[Sixt Kargel]

Tuning: bB gG dD gG d'd' e'e'

142

[43] Tu sai madonna

[Orlando di Lasso]
[Sixt Kargel]

Tuning: bB gG dD gG d'd' e'e'

Intabulations for Keyboard

[44] La cortesia

Orlande [de Lassus]
[Anon.]

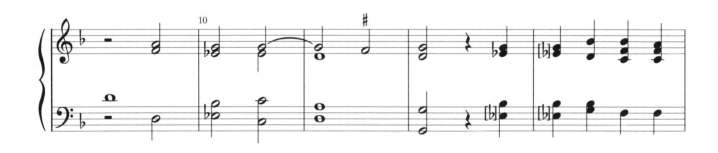

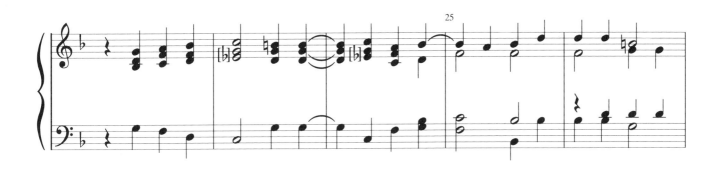

[45] No giorno

Orlande de Lassus
[Anon.]